To all those who support me daily

Contents

wetter than mine has been for months. Once I finish with this case, I need to spend an evening with a woman in the Disorderly House.

Many decades ago, it was determined the members of The Famiglia needed a place to go and safely fuck without fear of disease, pregnancy, or blackmail. It is open to both single and married male members. The Famiglia hired only the most beautiful women with bodies made for sin. They were fully vetted, and each one underwent extensive physicals, which included an IUD. The Famiglia pays the women well, and they live rent-free in an apartment building owned by The Famiglia.

Before engaging in any activities, members must meticulously read and sign the strict rules imposed by The Famiglia. Each room is equipped with panic alarms, a constant reminder of the consequences of breaking their ironclad laws. Any member who dares to defy these rules will be swiftly apprehended by The Famiglia guards and thrown into a grim holding cell, awaiting their inevitable trial and brutal punishment.

Each woman in the house fills out a detailed questionnaire that lists the activities they are willing to participate in. Some want only to do traditional sexual acts, while others like to be dominated or different types of fetish activities. The woman I choose has to enjoy pain and willingness to submit completely to my dark desires. I'm not a tender lover. Sex is raw without feelings.

I know I have been putting off selecting a wife. Frankly, the single women in the New York branch of the Famiglia are not up to my standards. There are branches all over the world, but the five founding families are here in New York. As a founding son, I have to pick a daughter of a member to be my wife. Since my station is the upper echelon, her station cannot be much lower than mine and she must be pure.

Girls raised inside The Famiglia are taught from a young

age to remain pure. Before the wedding, she will be subject to a virginity exam by one of The Famiglia doctors. During the exam, a member of The Commission, the governing body of The Familia, will be a witness. As a founding son, I have the right to select who would be a witness from The Commission. I know it is impossible, but I would prefer a woman who hasn't even been around another male unless it is their father or brother. I don't trust uncles or male cousins, and don't even get me started with male teachers or male students. Horny bastards are what they are.

As I think about such a woman, my cock hardens and I find myself thinking about how I would take her repeatedly. She would learn quickly how to swallow my cock, take it deep in her virginal pussy, and up her tight asshole. Damn, I needed to stop thinking these thoughts and concentrate on the job at hand.

I hope Charles understands the severity of becoming a member of Famiglia. Today was the last step in the process. The Famiglia wanted Charles for his expertise in AI technology. It was the way of the future, and we need him to prepare us for whatever it may bring.

Charles Greco's background wasn't the only one that I went through, but also his family. Other than his daughter, he was the last living Greco. His son died at the age of seven, riding his bike in front of his home. The driver didn't stop, and the cops never found them. Five years later, his wife was killed by a drunk driver as she and their infant daughter were coming home from the hospital after her birth. The driver of both vehicles both died as well. However, the infant survived.

His daughter, Angelina, was an enigma. The only information I could find was her date of birth and she was homeschooled. There were no hospital or doctor records at any office within a fifty-mile radius. I also couldn't find one picture or social media post about her. This bothers me. What near twenty-one-year-old doesn't have social media? Also, why wasn't I finding any photos? Was she injured during the accident? Was she disfigured or scared? Maybe today I would find answers to my questions because it wasn't just Charles who was joining The Famiglia, but Angelina as well.

She would be subject to rules and regulations as much as her father, even more so. Females of The Famiglia did not have any rights. Before they were married, their father was in charge of every aspect of their life. They are raised to become subservient to their future husbands. Men of the Famiglia are heads of the household and are dominant in all aspects of their wives and daughters' lives. We dictate what they wear, whom they speak to, where they go, what they read, what music they listen to, and most importantly, when we have sex. Any time, day or night, our wives must spread their legs for their husbands, no matter where they were. They also must remain faithful to their husbands. The Famiglia rule of a woman's infidelity is quite severe. Once found guilty, their husband takes them to the punishment circle in front of The Famiglia compound. There, they are chained to the whipping post, stripped bare, and their husband would give them twenty lashes with a whip. Members of The Famiglia stand around the couple and bear witness to her punishment.

When The Famiglia decided they wanted Charles as a potential member, they sent me to begin the process. The first meeting was where I could get a feeling of Charles. During the meeting, I left breadcrumbs of The Famiglia, which would either make Charles intrigued or not.

Of course, his analogical brain wanted to know more. After he signed a stringent NDA, he was given the history of The Famiglia and the reason why they wanted him to become part. I loved the look on his face when we told him who was a member of The Famiglia. It is not every day you find out that the President of the United States is part of a secret organization.

The next stage required a substantial non-refundable

payment to The Famiglia. Once that was done, Charles received a copy of the rules and regulations, as well as the ceremonies within The Famiglia. Charles asked several questions, but nothing out of the ordinary. He didn't ask any questions concerning his daughter becoming a daughter of The Famiglia or the rules she must follow.

My car comes to a stop in front of the Greco home. It is a large Victorian Mansion built in the mid-1800s. The Greco family immigrated from Italy in the early 1800s and settled in this location. I wonder if Charles knew his family's history before they immigrated. The Greco family once had an opportunity to be one of the founding families. However, just before the alliance was formed, Marcus Greco was killed in a tragic accident. The heir to the family was his infant son and he couldn't make the alliance due to his age.

My driver and security, Hamm, opens the back door, and I exit. I straighten my Alexander Amosu suit jacket and ensure my Kimber 1911 45 is secure in my shoulder holster. All founding sons, their families, and faces of family leaders receive security details. Hamm is my primary guard, but I also have a contingent of guards at my disposal. If I ever need extra support, I only have to call The Famiglia for assistance.

I walk up to the door and ring the bell. Moments later, a woman dressed in a black dress opens the door. From my notes, this was one of many female staff Charles has on his payroll. Most of the staff live in private living quarters in the rear of the home.

"Mr. Genovese, sir, welcome. Mr. Greco is waiting in the living room for you."

I nod in agreement and follow her graceful strides down the long hall, my Italian leather shoes clicking along the polished wooden floor. As I glance around, my eyes are drawn to the stunning artwork lining the walls. Each piece is a masterpiece of colors and textures, but I am unable to recognize the painter. Nevertheless, I appreciate the beauty they bring to the space. The woman stops at a doorway, standing off to the side and gesturing for me to enter.

Charles stands as I come in. "Mr. Genovese, please come in and have a seat."

"Thank you, Mr. Greco," I say, taking a seat on the leather sofa. Once seated, Charles takes his seat across from me in a tall leather chair. His manners please me and will please The Famiglia. A moment later, the woman returns, carrying a silver tray with a whiskey decanter and two glasses. She places the tray on the table and quickly exits.

Charles pours two tumblers half full of the rich amber liquid. "I hope you like bourbon."

"I do, thank you."

We both take a generous drink. The expensive liquor burns a path in my throat in the most enjoyable way. I know the taste. It was expensive bourbon, Angel's Envy. I have several bottles in my liquor cabinet in my home office. I lean back and look at Charles. "Do you have questions before we continue the process?"

He sits down the glass, I can't help but notice how his hand shook and faltered for just a second. It was the first time I had seen him look shaken. My instincts kick in and I feel a sense of unease wash over me.

"Mr. Genovese, I want to join The Famiglia, but I have a request before I sign," he says.

So he wants to negotiate. "Mr. Greco, the payment is non-negotiable, as are the rules and regulations."

He shakes his head. "I don't have a problem with the money or the rules. This involves my daughter, Angelina."

His words catch me off guard. The unexpectedness of it all sends my thoughts into a whirlwind, questioning Charles' motives for hiding Angelina from the world. "What about her?" I ask as I try to steady my voice.

"First, let me properly introduce you to her," Charles replies with a calm demeanor as if he's done this many times before.

My curiosity is piqued, and I eagerly await the revelation of this secret individual. "Okay," I say, my heart beating faster with anticipation and intrigue.

Charles pulls out his phone. "Please tell Angelina we are ready."

"As you know, we do an extensive background check on you and your family. How have you kept your daughter from the public?" I ask.

"I'll explain everything after you meet her," Charles says as he looks toward the doorway.

I turn just as the most stunningly beautiful woman walks into the room. Never in my life had I ever seen anyone like her. She was ethereal, like an angel stepping down from heaven. I watch as she walks, no floats, toward her father and hugs him.

"Mr. Genovese, I am honored to introduce you to my daughter, Angelina."

My breath caught when she turns.

Angelina was a goddess among mortals. Her skin was a canvas of milky white that seemed to glow in the soft light, inviting to be touched. Her hair cascaded down her back like spun gold. The mesmerizing intensity of her eyes, deep pools of sapphire, reflected the world around her in a symphony of colors. Standing tall and regal, her presence exuded a comforting warmth that tingled upon contact. Angelina possessed a figure that could only be described as divine, with generous breasts, a small waist, and hips that swayed with a tantalizing curve. But it was her smile, a harmonious blend of joy and contentment, that truly stole hearts. It was warm and radiant, like the embrace of a gentle breeze on a summer day, illuminating her face with a natural glow. Without a doubt, she was the most beautiful woman I had ever laid eyes on.

As she stands before me, my hand desperately longs to reach out and brush my hand against her face to verify her reality. But an instinctual dread clutches at me, whispering that any contact would shatter the illusion, dissipating her like a fleeting mirage.

Every inch of my body tingles with eager anticipation as she gracefully takes a deliberate step toward me. The pounding of my heart echoes in my ears, overpowering any other sound. The air is so heavy with the scent of anticipation and nervousness, as if we were suspended in a moment of undeniable connection. She stood still, mere inches away from me, her intense gaze locking onto mine. It was as if her gaze was consuming my entire existence, leaving me feeling empty.

"Mr. Genovese," she says, her voice soft and melodious. "I am honored to meet you."

I extend my arm, hand cautiously grasps her delicate

hand, savoring the velvety sensation of her skin. A gentle warmth emanates from her touch, causing a soothing shiver to travel up my arm. Our hands intertwine as if our souls merge, forging an indestructible connection.

"It's my pleasure," I say, my voice hoarse with emotions.

She smiles, and my heart skips several beats.

"As it is mine, Mr. Genovese," she says.

"Please call me Giovanni," I say, enjoying the electrical current flowing between us, yet confused about why that was.

We stand there for a moment, just looking at each other. I feel I could stay like this forever. What the fuck? I have never reacted to a woman like this before. But I need to know everything about her. All her secrets and all her desires would be mine to know.

Then she releases my hand, and I feel the warmth of her touch slip away. I watch her go, and I know I will never forget her. As she leaves the room, she glances back at me, her face blushing with a pink hue. Damn, I wonder if that pink hue breaks out on other parts of her body.

After she leaves, I look back to Charles. Pure joy radiates on his face, yet a subtle trace of fear lingers in his eyes. With a subtle gesture, he asks me to sit down. We take our seats again, and he pours a generous amount of bourbon into our waiting glasses. I pick up my glass and down the entire contents.

"What do you want from me?" I ask.

Charles takes a deep breath. "I am aware The Famiglia has dug into my life. However, I am sure they did not find my nightmare."

"Nightmare?" I ask, confused by his statement.

Charles looks at the ceiling before looking back at me. "It all started when I had a breakthrough in a program for the banking system. Jimmy was seven and was pitching for his first Little League team. He was great, if I have to say so myself. One day, I sat at one of his ball games, and a man sat beside me. I didn't pay any attention to him until he said my name. I looked toward him and recognized him from the papers. He was Mateo Cruz, the drug kingpin of the Cuban Corporation."

"Mateo Cruz?" I ask. I knew who Cruz was, and the Cuban Corporation was one of The Famiglia's enemies.

"Yes. He said he wanted me to use my breakthrough to hack into world banks and filter drug money to be laundered. I told him I couldn't do that, and one week later, they killed Jimmy as he rode his bike."

"You think Mateo killed Jimmy?"

"I know so. At the graveside, I saw him standing beside a tree with a smug look on his face. I contacted the FBI and told them my story. However, they didn't believe me. So, I did everything possible to protect my wife. The years went by, and Mateo never contacted me again. I thought maybe he gave up on me, but I was so wrong. It wasn't until later I discovered he had been arrested and sent to jail for five years."

"My beautiful Cecilia became pregnant once again. We were so excited, and when Angelina was born, it was the happiest day in our lives since Jimmy's death. I was ready to bring them home when I got an emergency call from work telling me someone had broken into my lab and trashed everything. Cecilia told me to go check it out, and she would take Angelina home and wait for me. After ordering another car, I kissed her, told her I loved her, and rushed out of the hospital. When I arrived at my lab, I found the damage. I knew my data was backed up, so I wasn't worried about that, but it was still heartbreaking to see the damage. I sat down at my desk and it was then I saw the picture. It was of Cecilia and me walking into the hospital with a red cross on Cecilia's swollen belly. I jumped to my feet and ran to my car, yelling at my driver to hurry home. A mile away from the house, I saw the flashing of police lights and I knew I was too late. I jumped from the car and ran toward the lights."

I listen, stunned by the tale. Charles picks up his glass and takes a large drink. How had this information gotten past me?

"As soon as I saw the car, I knew there was no way anyone could survive. However, I needed to see for myself. I tried to get closer, but the officers wouldn't let me near. I dropped to my knees and sobbed. When I thought all was lost, I heard a sweet baby cry. A paramedic came over, carrying Angelina in their arms. They bent down and placed her in my arms. I swore then I would protect her at all costs. After bringing her home, I gave Mateo the program, but not until I added a tracking routine. Five years after the first transaction, it would transmit all data of its activities to the FBI. I also erased all data that would tie me to the program, as well as all the information other than basics on my son's and wife's deaths. I am sure you heard he was found guilty of federal charges and is sitting in federal prison for twenty to life. I was still scared something would happen to Angelina, so I kept her here in our home for the last twenty-one years. She had tutors and physicians who came to the house. I made sure all of them were female and of Italian descent. I took no chance that Mateo would try to get one of his men in the house. When you came and proposed that I join The Famiglia, it was the first time I slept an entire night in over twenty-five years. When I was younger, my grandfather told me about our family's missed opportunity because of a tragic death. The opportunity was The Famiglia, wasn't it?"

I couldn't confirm or deny his question until he signed the contract. "Charles, before I answer, I need to know if you have decided to join The Famiglia?"

"I have, but I have a request before I sign," Charles says, looking me in the eye.

"As I stated before, the money, rules, and regulations are non-negotiable."

"I know you want my technology in AI, and I hope it was worth my request," he says.

No one ever requested something before signing. At the point of the recruitment, the person was aware of what was required of them. I know how much The Famiglia wants Charles, and as a founding son, I could make concessions.

"What is the request?"

"I want you to marry Angelina."

My breath hitches. Of all the things he could have requested, this was not one I would have ever guessed. Yes, The Famiglia wants Charles, but I am a founding son. I must choose my wife, who is part of the upper echelon. I am about to tell Charles to take his request and stick it up his ass when I see a photo of Angelina on the mantle behind Charles's head. She is everything I have thought I would want in a wife. She is untouched by the world. My mind races as I think of her milky white skin glistening on the ceremonial snow-white sheets as I bury my cock deep inside of her virginal pussy. I can almost hear her cries of both pain and ecstasy as she comes on my dick. Then an image of me fucking her mouth, forcing my cock down her throat, as she tries to breathe.

If Charles knew my thoughts and my inclinations, of my desires and tastes toward sex, he wouldn't offer me his pure, angelic daughter. Has he not read about the section on marriage ceremonies?

Members of The Famiglia and the founding sons have rules when they wed. All members of The Famiglia must marry in the church on the compound. After the ceremony, they take their bride to the ceremonial dais in the center of the compound. The founding five families and the four elected consigliere, which make up the governing body of The Famiglia, called The Commission, surround the couple. They place her on the ceremonial bench and cuff her hands and ankles to the bench. Her husband will then mark her body with a tattoo over her heart, linking her to her husband.

If the member doesn't have a family crest, they use the crest of The Family. Each founding family has a unique symbol of their family, which is part of their family crest. The Genovese was, of course, the dragon. I already have the design ready for when I select my wife. It is a black dragon's face with fiery red eyes and my initials. I am the dragon and my dark soul will drag her from her heavenly light tower to burn under my rule. After she is tattooed, she pledges her allegiance to her husband, kneeling at his feet and kissing his ring. In Italian, she states Padrone del mio cuore, corpo e anima, Master of my heart, body, and soul.

What would others think about me marrying someone who just joined The Famiglia? I am Giovanni Drago Genovese and I can have any woman I want, even if she is promised to someone else. The woman I marry will be royalty inside The Famiglia. Women and young girls in our society will look to her for direction on how they should dress and act. Fuck, was I considering this? I need to be sure Charles understands what is involved if I am to marry his daughter.

"Charles, I need to be certain you understand what you are asking me. There are specific rites to the ceremony for the marriage of a member of The Famiglia. Also, marrying Angelina doesn't just make her my wife. It makes her my submissive. I can do anything to her. I can do anything I want to her body. From her neck to her toes. I will fuck her mouth, cunt, ass, and tits. I can whip, spank, bind her to my bed, and do or use anything else I desire on her body. And the best part is I don't need your permission. Once you agree to the wedding, she is mine. If I want to fuck her until she is a quivering mass of flesh in my bed, I can."

I finish my statement. The room fills with an awkward silence as I anxiously await Charles's response, wondering if he has reconsidered his offer of his daughter. He must grasp the fact that this is my genuine nature.

Moments pass by, and the only sounds in the room are our breathing and the tick of the clock. I stare at Charles's face, trying to read his thoughts. I see he is taking in all that I have disclosed about my inclinations towards sex and what it is like to be a wife of a member of The Famiglia.

"But will she be safe?" He asks. "Will the Cuban Corporation or any other person hurt her?"

The very idea of someone else being with her or causing her harm fills me with an intense fury, my blood pulsating with a familiar rage. "I will burn the world to ash if anyone touches her other than me."

"Then do you agree to marry her?" he asks.

"She is mine," I state.

"Then where do we place the agreement on the contract?" Charles asks.

"We don't. This is not an agreement between The Famiglia and you. It is between the two of us," I say.

I can feel his intense scrutiny as he furrows his brow, examining my face. Just as he begins to speak, I instinctively raise my hand to halt him, already aware of his thoughts.

"I am Giovanni Drago Genovese, a founding son of The Famiglia and the leader of the Genovese crime family. When I give you my word that I will marry Angelina, it means it will happen."

"But why not put it on the agreement?"

"Because I don't want members below me to think I lowered my standard for a wife because The Famiglia wanted your expertise. Nothing is perfect, and that includes The Famiglia. I don't want anyone to say anything negative about Angelina. We will do this the way they have done it for centuries."

"And how is that?"

"She turns twenty-one in five days, correct?" I ask.

"Yes," he answers, still with a confused look on his face.

"Then this whirlwind relationship will happen in five days. I will return here tomorrow at eleven-thirty to pick Angelina up to take her to lunch," I say.

"But she has never been off the estate," he says. I see the genuine fear in his eyes and he has every right to be so. The fucking Cubans are ruthless motherfuckers but I am a hundred times worse.

"Well, that changes now. We need to be seen together as a couple, and it starts with us eating lunch at one of my restaurants. There, I can control security, and with it being Tuesday, I know the restaurant will be filled with some of the biggest busybodies in town. The rumor mill will begin immediately, and by nightfall, everyone who is anyone will want to know who she is and why she is with me," I explain.

"I don't understand why it must be this way," Charles says.

"Because they have not seen me in public with a woman. If we are to weave the tale of how I couldn't wait to marry her, we must put on this production."

"What happens after lunch?" He asks.

"They will see us in public as much as possible. On Thursday, I will put a ring on her finger. That evening is an event at The Famiglia compound. We will attend the event together, and that includes you. I will announce our engagement there and hold our wedding on Saturday evening in the chapel."

Charles's eyes darted around, and he rubbed his hands together. It was a sign he was nervous about something.

"What is it, Charles?"

"How do I," he started but stopped. His eyes drifted towards the doorway. He was trying to figure out how to tell Angelina she would marry me.

"Have you explained to her the rules of The Famiglia and what they will expect of her when she marries a member?" I asked.

"I explained some of it to her. However, when I told her about how the men of The Famiglia are head of household and in charge of everything in their wives' lives, she surprised me with the statement. *Do you mean like a dominant and submissive lifestyle?"*

"How does she know about BDSM?" I growl. I thought she was sheltered in this home.

"She said she read about it online," he answers.

"Well, that is mostly just shit bad romance authors use in their smut novels. She has no clue what it means to be in a truly subservient relationship. I hope she doesn't think that will be the type of relationship we will have. I am the master. What I say goes without delay or argument."

"I will talk to her," Charles says.

I shake my head at him. "No, you won't. The moment you agreed to give me your daughter, you lost all rights to her. I will tell her. Now, let's finish the paperwork so I can go home and start planning our wedding."

Charles closes his eyes for a moment before nodding and standing.

"I am ready to give my pledge," he says.

Seeing him stand, I knew he had read the information concerning this ceremony. I reach into my jacket and pull out the ring he would wear after pledging his allegiance to The Famiglia. "Charles, you may begin."

"I, Charles Leonard Greco, do hereby commit myself and my family to The Famiglia. I pledge to honor and serve The Famiglia until my dying breath. I swear to keep all its secrets and sacrifice anything for its success. I vow to protect its members, uphold its traditions, and execute its wishes without question or hesitation. May God strike me dead if I ever betray The Famiglia."

I nod my approval and place the ring on Charles's finger. It fit him perfectly, as I knew it would. His eyes sparkled with newfound pride, and I could see he was eager to prove his worth to The Famiglia. I pull out the contract and sit it on the table. "Once you sign this, you and your family will be in The

Famiglia. You will gain all the privileges and security as a member."

Charles picks up the pen and signs his name on the line. Once he is finished, I turn the document toward me and sign as the witness. I pick it up and place it back in my case.

"Charles, to answer your questions, yes, it was The Famiglia. Your family was going to be one of the founding leaders. It might have taken a while, but from here on out, your family and children's families will be part of The Famiglia."

A sadness falls over his face. "My only family will be a Genovese."

I place a hand on his arm. "You never know where life might have in store for you."

"Thank you, Mr. Genovese."

"Charles, we are about to become family. You can call me Giovanni."

"Thank you, Giovanni. Let me walk you to the door."

We make our way out of the cozy living room and down the warm lite hallway. As we pass a series of paintings, I pause at one with bold, abstract shapes and colors. The brushstrokes seem to dance across the canvas, drawing me in with their chaotic yet captivating energy. A sense of darkness lingers within the painting, but there is also a glimmer of hope as a sliver of light tries to break through the shadows. I am trans-fixed by the piece and find myself searching for the signature of the talented artist.

"Do you like the painting?" Charles asks.

"Yes. Who is the artist?"

"Angelina."

I was stunned. She was very talented.

"I did not know she painted," I say.

"She is quite gifted," Charles says with a proud smile on his face. "I know she will make you a wonderful wife."

I nod, my mind consumed by the painting, a reflection of

her, I realize, with a surge of possessiveness. The darkness surrounding her life, sheltered and secluded from the world, was captured in the brushstrokes. But a sliver of light represented someone coming to protect her. And that someone was me. I vow to provide for her every desire, to control and mold her into the perfect partner for my criminal empire. She will belong to me, completely and utterly, and precisely how I want it to be.

We reach the front door, and I turn to Charles. "I'll see you tomorrow at eleven-thirty. I will have a messenger bring her the dress, shoes, and accessories."

"She has lots of beautiful dresses," Charles states.

"From this moment forward, she only dresses in clothes I select for her."

"Yes, Giovanni. I'm sorry to have questioned you."

"I will let it pass this time. However, I don't give second chances."

I walk down the steps and climb into the car. I think about what just happened as Hamm drives back toward the city. When I came here this evening, it was to bring in a new member to The Famiglia. We have a new member, but I also came out with a future wife. Fuck, I can't believe I am getting married. This was going to be a shock to the members of The Famiglia and to my close friends, the other founding sons.

Thankfully, I can say I met her months ago when I first met with Charles. I wanted to keep our relationship secret until her father signed the contract. Damn, I have so much to arrange.

I grab my phone and call Davide. He is another of the founding sons, the head of the Bonanno crime family and someone I trusted.

"Gio. Did you get Greco to sign?"

"Yes. We officially have a new member and access to his groundbreaking AI technology."

"That is great. Do you want to celebrate? I can meet you at The Den."

Even though I have a list mile-long, a drink sounded good. "Yeah. I should be there in about thirty minutes. Go ahead up to the VIP section and start without me."

"Alright. Do you want me to round up some female company?" he asks.

Every fiber in my being screams for female company, especially after months of going without some pussy. Even though I am getting married in five days, I could enjoy the evening balls deep in another woman's pussy and nothing would be said. In The Famiglia, women must be loyal to their husbands, while the husbands can indulge in many sexual partners. As I open my mouth to accept the offer, a vivid image of Angelina's blushing face fills my mind. No other woman could come close to her divine beauty. With that thought, a wave of guilt and longing washes over me, and I manage to choke out, "Not tonight." My inner turmoil threatens to consume me as I resist the temptation and cling to my vows.

"Alright, I see you there," Davide says.

I put my phone back and wonder what the fuck I am doing. No way was I going to allow her to rule me. I am the lord and master of my home and everything that pertains to Angelina. I search through my contacts and call my cousin Anna. She is my father's late brother's daughter and is five years younger than me.

"Gio, so good to hear from you," Anna says.

"I've been busy."

"Always working too hard and not taking time to enjoy life."

"You are right. I am calling because I need you to do something for me, and I know I can trust you to keep it a secret."

"Of course you can."

"I need you to pick up several dresses that would be

perfect for a lunch date, as well as everything else that would accompany them. Bring them to the estate no later than eight tomorrow morning."

"Gio, it is nine o'clock!" She exclaims. "Where do you think I will get anything at this hour?"

"Anna, I know you have several high-end boutique owners on speed dial. You forget I pay your monthly credit card bills, which are big enough to feed a small country," I say with a chuckle. It is true. Anna's father left her, her mother, and her sister very well off. However, she couldn't control her money because she was a daughter of The Famiglia. When my father made me the Boss of the Genovese family, I assumed the responsibility of handling their inheritance.

"Damn it, I do, but why do you need women's clothes? Gio, you haven't switched sides, have you?" she giggles.

"Anna," I growl.

Her breath catches and a cold, calculating smile spreads across my face. Anna finally realizes the power I hold over her and her family. With her father dead and no male heirs, I am now the sole ruler of this household, controlling every aspect of their lives, from finances to their behaviors. If they dare to disobey or challenge me, they face swift and severe punishment. My list of rules is not to be taken lightly. In fact, I have already had to strap each one of them to my whipping bench at least once, watching with twisted pleasure as I set their flesh on fire with each punishing strike.

"I'm sorry, Giovanni," she whispers.

"Better. What I am about to tell you must remain a secret between us. This includes your mother, sister, or anyone you might speak to. Do you understand?"

"Yes, Gio, I understand."

"Good. I'm getting married, and I need to build my future wife's wardrobe until we go together to select clothes," I say.

"Married?" she squeaks.

"Yes," I answer. This was probably the response from everyone as they learn about the engagement.

"Okay. What are her sizes, and what color do you want me to avoid?"

"Shit," I grumble. I forgot to get the information from Charles. "I will text you her sizes. Stay away from bold colors. I want nothing to revealing or overly tight, but don't make her look like a nun."

"Okay. I'll call my friend, and as soon as I get the sizes, I'll go to the shop and pick out several dresses," Anna says. "And Giovanni, congratulations. She must be exceptional for you to pick her as your wife."

"She is," I say before I can catch myself. I hang up and quickly call Charles.

"Giovanni," he answers on the second ring.

"Charles, I need Angelina's sizes, including shoe sizes."

"Oh, of course. She is a size six, and her shoe size is seven."

"Thank you." I hang up before he can respond.

After a quick text to Anna, I sit back and allow myself to envision her dressed in clothes I select for her.

I lean closer to Davide but fall forward and smack my forehead on the table. "Fuck, that hurts," I yelled, rubbing the spot. "She is Charles Greco's daughter."

"Gio, we are bound by duty and legacy as the founding sons," Davide says with a hard edge to his voice.

A hiccup leaves my lips. "Don't give a fuck. But I need you to be my second. However, keep your fucking eyes away from her pussy."

A fiery rage consumes me as I glare at Davide's mocking expression. My fist clenches tightly, instinctively aiming for his jaw, but he effortlessly ducks my swing. The force of my attack sends me hurtling towards the couch and table, crashing to the floor in a heap. As I lay there, seething with anger and humiliation, I hear Davide's laughter ringing in my ears. He grabs me roughly and hauls me back onto the couch, grinning sadistically as he shakes his head in amusement.

"I would never look at something that wasn't mine. I promise to make sure Angelina is comfortable and secure during the process," he says.

"Thanks, man," I say.

"Alright, I've got to piss. Are you going to be okay by yourself?" he asks.

I pat my side where my gun was. "Yeah, man." I lean back on the couch and allow the sultry music to pour over me. I wonder what Angelina is doing right now. Damn, I didn't get to hear her soft, sensual voice enough. I need to hear it NOW. Pulling out my phone and scroll through my contacts. Why the fuck can't I find her name? DAMN IT! How had I not gotten her phone number? I scroll down, I push Charles's number.

Two rings later, he answers, his voice gravely. "Giovanni?"

"Charles, I need to talk to Angelina," I demand.

I hear rustling and wonder if Charles has been asleep. "It is after one o'clock in the morning, Giovanni. She is asleep."

"I DON'T FUCKING CARE!" I yell. "Give me her phone number."

"She doesn't have a phone," he says.

"Then take your phone to her to. I'll rectify the phone situation tomorrow. I will access her at all times, no matter what time, day or night. Do I make myself clear?"

A moment of silence before Charles answers. "Yes."

I listen as he must be getting out of bed and hear him walking. After what seems like an eternity, I hear a soft knock on a door.

"Angelina," he whispers.

Then I hear it. The sweet voice of the woman who was mine. "Daddy, is there something wrong?" The worry in her voice was evident.

"No, sweetheart. Ahh, Giovanni wants to speak with you."

"Oh," she says. Was that excitement in her voice?

"Charles, leave after handing over the phone," I command. I don't want him to listen to our conversation. This was a private conversation between Angelina and me.

"Giovanni, I understand who you are, but as her father, I also have a responsibility to protect her," he says in a voice more authoritative than I had heard before from him.

"You are her father. However, the position as her husband outranks you. So leave the phone and get the fuck out of her bedroom."

He huffs. "Fine."

I wait until I hear her door close before saying anything. "Angelina?"

In a feather-light voice. "Mr. Genovese."

I hate not hearing my first name coming from her lips. "NO!" I snap. "You call me Giovanni."

"Okay," she says cautiously.

"Angelina, say my name," I command through the fog of rage and alcohol.

"Giovanni," she says so quietly that I almost didn't hear it over the music in the background.

"Better," I say, picking up the tumbler and drinking. "What are you doing?"

"Ahh, sleeping."

I look at my Rolex and see it is, in fact, one-thirty in the morning. "What a good little girl you are all snuggled up in bed. Were you dreaming, little girl?"

"Ahh, yes," she stammers.

"Tell me about it."

"I can't," she says, hearing the rustling of sheets. Was she aroused? Was she dreaming of me?

"You can and you will," I say. "Use your artistic mind and describe the dream in vivid detail, so if I close my eyes, I can see it just from your words."

"I can't do that. Please, Giovanni, don't make me."

"Was I in your dream?" I ask.

"Yes."

"What was I doing?"

"You were kissing me," she says.

"Oh, I can't wait to taste those lips. I bet they are so fucking sweet. Even though I am sure your other lips are even sweeter," I say, huskly.

She says nothing for a moment, and then I hear a gasp. She figured out the pink lips I could hardly wait to suck, bite, and ram my cock through. "Tell me, my angel."

"Well, we are kissing, and it turns hot. You run your hand over my breast, and you pinch my nipple hard. "

My cock grows in my pants as I picture Angelina whimpering at my touch. "What did you do?"

"Hehe, I scream out from the pain but it also feels good."

"I'm sure," I say. "What did you do next?"

"We are still kissing, and you are sucking my tongue into your mouth like you enjoyed it. I feel your hands on my breasts, and you are squeezing them."

"I wish I could be there to squeeze them in real life."

I love hearing Angelina's sultry voice. "Tell me more."

"Your hands start to travel down my body. When you get down to my pussy, your hand begins to rub and massage my clit."

My breathing picks up. I close my eyes and visualize Angelina in my bed as I touch her. "Are you wet, my angel?"

"Yes."

"Are you afraid of what is going to happen?"

"No."

"Why is that, Angelina?"

"Because I want it to happen," she says as if she actually has some control. That shit would never happen. I am her lord and master, and I control every aspect of her life.

"Do you want it to hurt?"

"Ahh, no."

"I'm sure you are lying again. I bet your cunt is wet for me just at the thought of the pain."

"Ahh, no."

"Don't ever lie to me," I command. "If I ever catch you lying, I will turn you over my knee, no matter where we are, pull down your panties and spank your ass until it is glowing red. "

"You want to spank me?" she asks in a little voice.

"Yes, so much so."

"Giovanni, I have never done anything like this before," she admits.

"You better have not," I say. "All your first belong to me."

"Why me?" she asks, but before I can answer, I see Davide walking back to the area. What had Charles told her about me?

"Don't touch yourself, sleep well, and be ready at eleven-thirty," I say. I smile as I hang up, knowing I left Angelina wet and needy.

It was late, and I needed to get home. Tomorrow was the

first day Angelina had been outside her estate, and I needed to ensure she knew she was safe. I can't imagine what it is like to have never been around people other than your family and loyal staff.

I stand as Davide nears. "Hey man, it's late, and I have a full day tomorrow. I need to drink a shit load of water to try to sober up so I don't have a fucking hangover. Maybe we can get together before the exam so she can get to know you."

Davide's mouth turns up. "Who the fuck are you, and what have you done with The Dragon?"

I swing at him, and this time, I connect with his jaw. He reaches up and rubs where my fist hit. "The Dragon is still here, asshole."

He lets out a laugh and slaps me on the back. "Call me, and I can't wait to meet Angelina."

As I leave the club alone, a cold realization dawns on me. I have been using women as disposable objects, fulfilling my own needs without ever considering theirs. Each time, I promise myself it will be different, but in the heat of the moment, I am consumed by selfish desires. But now, standing outside the club, I wonder if this is indeed what I want or if I am just trying to fill a void within myself.

I stumble towards the car where Hamm stands by the door with a patient, knowing look. My legs feel like lead, and it takes every ounce of strength I have to climb into the back seat. I can't help but wonder if this is my lifelong curse, never being able to find true happiness, no matter who I am with.

As the car pulls away from the club, I try to process the emotions swirling within me. I knew that I had a responsibility to Angelina to make sure she was safe and happy, but I couldn't help but feel like I was leading her into a world of darkness and deceit. I close my eyes and see her angelic face smiling at me.

What the hell is the buzzing noise? I try to open my eyes, but they feel like someone has poured sand into them. The buzzing continues, and I want to find out what it is, so I beat the hell out of it until it stops.

A soft knock sounds. "Mr. Genovese, sir."

Open my mouth, but my tongue is so fucking dry I can't speak. I finally get enough salvia to form. "Yes."

The door opens, and through the little bit my eyes can open, I see my housekeeper, Margaret, standing in the doorway. "Mr. Genovese, Miss Genovese is downstairs, sir, with the dresses."

With a groan, I force my bleary eyes to focus on the clock. Its bright red numbers mock me as they read 8 AM. I curse under my breath, feeling like absolute shit and unable to recall how I made it home last night, or was it early this morning?

"Mr. Hamm helped you upstairs, sir," Margaret says.

"Tell Anna I will be down in twenty minutes," I croak.

"Certainly, sir, and I'll have fresh coffee waiting for you."

Twenty minutes later, I am showered, dressed, and walking into the den, where Anna is waiting with a rack of dresses. "Morning, Anna."

"Good morning, Gio."

I sink into the plush cushions of my favorite red leather high-back chair. The familiar scent of coffee fills the air as Margaret gracefully hands me a steaming cup. "Thank you, Margaret."

"I'll have breakfast ready in twenty minutes. Would you like me to serve you here, sir?" she asks.

"Yes," I answer and turn towards Anna. "Show me what you brought."

I inspect each article of clothing with a critical eye. Anna's experience with lavish spending has clearly given her an edge in selecting the perfect dresses. After much consideration, I only reject two dresses and one pair of shoes. They were unsuitable for Angelina's skin tone. I kept going back and forth between two gorgeous dresses before deciding on the one that would make Angelina look flawless.

"You did a good job, Anna."

"Thank you, Gio. Do you need me to select more for her?"

"No. I am taking her shopping today."

"Okay. I can't wait to meet her," she says.

"Soon, I promise. Have a great rest of your day," I say, dismissing her.

After meticulously boxing up the dress and accessories, I sent Hamm to deliver the package to the Greco estate.

Now, I just have to wait until it is time to pick up my future.

Chapter Five

ANGELINA

I am so nervous I could throw up. Oh wait, I already did twice. It is eleven-twenty, and I am sitting in my room waiting for Giovanni to arrive for our date. I am going on my first date. Ordinary girls go on first dates all the time, but I'm not like ordinary girls because I am days away from my twenty-first birthday, and I have never left the estate. See, I'm not normal.

My life has never been normal. At first, I knew nothing differently. I thought all the little girls lived in a big house with their daddies. Mama went to heaven right after I was born, and I was told she was watching down on me. Daddy had teachers and doctors come to the estate to care for my learning and health needs.

It wasn't until I got old enough to have a computer that I realized what a freak I was. On my sixteenth birthday, I questioned Daddy about why I couldn't leave the estate. I could see the sadness and torment in his eyes. He broke down and told me everything. I couldn't believe there was so much evil in this world. If Daddy thought it was safer for me here, I was happy to stay. Undoubtedly, if something happened to me, Daddy wouldn't make it.

It was when I found art that I indeed found peace in the solitude of the estate. Daddy had an art studio designed for me and purchased everything a budding artist could ever wish for. I poured all my feelings into each piece I did.

About six months ago, I noticed a change in Daddy. He was spending more time on the computer, and I often caught him reading a large packet of papers. Then he came to me two weeks ago and explained that he was joining an organization that would give us more security. It was called The Famiglia. It was a secret society founded by five families in Italy centuries ago. He told me the rules he and I must follow to be part of The Famiglia. Men of The Famiglia are heads of household and are in charge of every aspect of the women in their lives. It reminded me a little of the alternative lifestyle I had read about. When I read about men dominating women not only in the bedroom but in everyday life, I felt it comforting.

Yesterday, Daddy told me he wanted to introduce me to a man who was one of the members of The Famiglia, Giovanni Drago Genovese. I was nervous to meet him because, other than my father, I had never been in a room with a man. The male guards are prohibited in the house unless it is a dire emergency. I've seen them from my window but never close up.

I wore my favorite dress and took special care of my hair and makeup.

When I heard a car pulling up, I couldn't help but take a peek from my window. Holy Cow! Giovanni is hot. The pictures on the internet didn't do him justice. Hazel came into my room, telling me it was time for me to come in. The moment I entered the room, all the air left my body. He had done nothing but stand, and I could feel his commanding presence all the way to my toes. Then, when our hands touched, I felt an electric current that went straight to my sex. My body shuttered, and my nipples grew hard. Was this what people felt before they had an orgasm? All too soon, I had to leave, but I couldn't help myself from taking one last look at him. I will never forget him and how he made me feel if I never saw him again.

Daddy came to my room after Giovanni left and told me he had asked me to accompany him to lunch. At first, I was excited. Then, as I thought about leaving the security of my home, I became nervous. Could I walk out the front door and get into a car? I didn't know I could, but the vision of Giovanni popped into my head. Daddy said he was joining The Famiglia for additional security. Would Giovanni protect me?

Left alone in the dark, I lay in bed, trying desperately to fall asleep. But the silence was deafening, and my mind couldn't help but wander to Giovanni, the forbidden fruit that tempted me. In a dreamlike state, he appeared before me, his lips crashing onto mine with an intensity I had never felt before. His hands roamed over my body, exploring every inch of me until they reached my pulsating sex. Just as he was about to fulfill my deepest desires, Daddy barged in and jolted me awake with his phone thrust into my hands, shattering the illusion and leaving me feeling empty and conflicted.

I couldn't believe Giovanni called me and somehow figured out I was having a sex dream about him. His voice made me want to tell him every detail of my dream. The words finally spilled out. Then he asked me if I liked pain, and I lied and said no. He must be a human lie detector because he immediately knew I had. He told me he wanted to spank me. I don't understand why it thrilled me, but it did. The thought of his enormous hand landing power smacks on my bare ass caused my panties to become sobbing wet. However, I was embarrassed. Did it make me even more of a freak? I was about to let my feeling of insecurity get the best of me, and then he reassured me by saying all my first was his.

I couldn't understand why he wanted me. It took everything. I had to ask him why. I thought he was going to tell me, but instead, he told me not to touch myself and to go to sleep. How did he know I needed to touch myself? And how the hell was I supposed to sleep when all my nerve endings were crackling?

I finally fell asleep, but my alarm clock went off too soon. Hazel brought up my breakfast tray. I could only get a few bites of eggs and toast before my stomach protested. I sipped on my coffee and tried to calm down. Where were we going?

After a long hot shower, I wondered what I was going to wear. I was going through my closet for the third time when Daddy came in with a large box. I asked Daddy what it was, and he told me it was what Giovanni wanted me to wear today. He picked out my outfit. It wasn't just my dress and shoes, but also lingerie. Oh my, I had worn nothing so sexy before. The Lacey panties were tiny and the bra barely covered my nipples.

At the bottom of the box was a new iPhone. When I turned it on, there was a text message from Giovanni.

> ANGELINA,
> THIS IS YOUR PHONE. KEEP IT CHARGED AND ON YOU AT ALL TIMES. NO MATTER WHAT YOU ARE DOING WHEN I CALL, YOU WILL ANSWER ME. BREAKING THESE RULES WILL RESULT IN A SORE ASS.
> GIOVANNI.

Shock coursed through my body, but it was quickly overshadowed by a primal arousal that I couldn't deny. My mind raced, trying to figure out how to survive this date without giving in to the fiery desire burning within me. The delicate fabric of my new panties felt like a ticking time bomb, threatening to give way at any moment under the relentless pressure building between my legs.

"Angelina."

I look up to find Daddy at my door.

"Yes, Daddy."

"Giovanni is here," he says.

I try to figure out the look on his face. It wasn't apprehension, but maybe sadness.

"Daddy, are you okay?" I ask, reaching out and taking his hand.

"Yes. I knew this day would come, but now that it is here, it just hit me."

"Daddy, it is just lunch."

"But this is the first time you have left the estate. I don't know how you can be so strong," he says.

"Oh, Daddy, I am so scared. However, you joined The Famiglia for extra security, and somehow, Giovanni wants to get to know me. I'm still trying to figure that out. I need to do this. We need this. It is time we both can live outside these walls."

He wraps his arms around me and squeezes me tight. "I am sorry I had to keep you here, but I couldn't lose you too. Giovanni is a powerful man who can move heaven on earth to keep what is safe. Remember the rules of The Famiglia. They are part of Giovanni, and he will not break them or allow anyone he has taken into his care to break them."

I collapse into my father's arms, tears streaming down my face as I soak in the overwhelming warmth and safety of his embrace. Today marked the start of my new life, finally free from the chains that held me prisoner for so long. My heart swells with a mix of relief and excitement, knowing that anything is now possible.

"Alright. Let's get you downstairs. I don't think Giovanni is a man you want to keep waiting," Daddy says with a chuckle.

He kisses me on the cheek and I pick up my purse, ensuring the phone is in it. Daddy offers me his arm, and we walk down the hall.

When we reach the top of the stairs, I glance down and see Giovanni. He is dressed in a navy blue suit custom-made to fit him perfectly, with a crisp white shirt and a blue striped tie. My heart flip-flops because I realize my dress complements his suit. Did he do it purposely?

As if sensing our presence, he turns, and our eyes meet. Even at this distance, I see what looks like fire in his dark brown, almost black, orbs. The intensity of his stare causes my knees to grow weak, and if my daddy didn't have my arm, I would surely collapse.

We make our way to the bottom of the stairs. Daddy releases his hold on me, and I take a few steps towards Giovanni. I stop in front of him with my head bowed. It is then I feel his hand under my chin.

His touch sends an electric shock through my body, igniting a fire in me that I can't control. He lifts my face, and I gasp at the look in his eyes. His eyes bore into mine with an intense hunger, causing my panties to become drenched with desire. My whole being ached for him, and I could barely resist the urge to drop to my knees and surrender myself completely. It would be effortless, giving in to his every demand and craving.

"Are you ready to go?" he asks.

"Yes, sir," I murmur.

He gives me a devilish grin, then turns to my father. "Charles, we will return later."

"Nowhere with supervision," Daddy says.

Giovanni narrows his eyes. "I will follow all the rules outlined by The Famiglia."

"Alright," Daddy says, his expression turns to a look of concern. "Keep her safe, please."

Giovanni wraps his arm around my waist and pulls me close. I breathe in his scent. It was a mixture of his expensive cologne and something that must be just him. It was intoxicating, and I could live the rest of my life doing it.

"With my life," Giovanni answers and ushers us out the door.

We walk outside, and I see a large black vehicle with a

Hearing her calling herself a weirdo makes my blood boil. I turn and capture her chin, turning it towards me. "If I ever hear you put yourself down again, I will turn you over my knee no matter where we are and spank your ass until it is red. Do you understand?"

As soon as the word spanking comes out of my mouth, her eyes grow large, and even though it is slight, I see her move her legs together. Hmm, the thought of a spanking turns her on. Well, well, well, this is a surprise.

"Yes, sir," she says as she tries to lower her face. However, I still have her chin and hold her face still.

"Don't be ashamed. I will guide you on how I want things. As long as you follow my rules, I will award you. But break my rules, and there will be dire consequences." She nods her head, and pink tongues come out, licking her lips. Damn, I want to suck that tongue. I lean forward, and just as my lips are about to touch hers, a tap comes to the window. There would be no way I could just stop once I tasted those lips. I move over and kiss her cheek instead. "Stay put," I tell her and open my door.

Scanning the area, I saw that all the security was in place and was ready for Angelina to exit. Hamm walks with me around the car and opens the back door. I reach in, and Angelina puts her hand in mine. Her long, slender leg emerges, and she steps out. I hold out my arm, and she wraps hers around it. We walk arm and arm to the front door of the restaurant. Hamm opens the door and we walk in.

Jillian rushes over, her heels clicking against the polished floors of the restaurant. "Mr. Genovese, your table is ready, sir," she announces, undressing with her eyes. Damn it. I had forgotten that she worked during lunch. Whenever I see her, she throws herself at me like an eager puppy seeking attention. As if I would ever give her the time of day, let alone stick my cock in her. Angelina clutches my arm tighter, possessively marking her territory. I can't help but smile at the fury in her eyes as she shoots daggers at Jillian's back. Her jealousy is almost endearing.

We follow Jillian through the restaurant, and as we walk by the tables, I can hear the murmurs of the ladies. Angelina seems to notice as well and clings onto my arm even tighter. I can feel her body tense, knowing she is not used to being in the spotlight. I make a mental note to ensure she has more exposure to social situations like this. She must hold her own, especially if she will be my wife.

As we approach our table, the chatter in the restaurant subsides, and all eyes are on us. I can see the calculating looks of the women, sizing up Angelina and me. I can almost hear their thoughts, speculating on our relationship and how we came together.

I pull out Angelina's chair and help her sit before taking my seat. Jillian hands Angelina her menu and then mine. Her finger brushes against the back of my hand. "What can I get you to drink?" she asks in a husky voice.

"A bottle of Gaja Barbaresco," I say, never taking my eyes off Angelina. Jillian huffs and stomps off.

As we perused the menu, I could feel Angelina's eyes on me.

"Is everything all right?"

"Yes, sir. I'm just wondering what all these people are staring at us."

"They are all wondering who you are and why you are here with me."

"Why would they wonder that?"

"Because you are the first woman I have been seen with in public."

"Ever?" she asks.

"Yes. My cousin usually goes with me when I have to go to functions in the evening."

Jillian comes back with our wine. "I will let you know when we are ready to order," I dismiss her.

I can practically feel the waves of tension emanating from Angelina's body. Her shoulders are so tightly bunched up that I worry they might snap. Her eyes dart frantically around the room, scanning for potential danger. Without hesitation, I grab her trembling hand and squeeze it firmly. But instead of finding comfort in my touch, she flinches as if she's been burned. "Relax," I command, my voice laced with steely determination. "You are under my protection now. No one will dare to lay a finger on you while you are with me."

Angelina takes a deep breath and lets it out slowly. Her shoulders relax. "I'm trying, but it's hard. I'm not used to this."

" I don't want you to be distressed. You don't have to be anything other than who you are. Would you like me to order for you?" I ask.

"Please, sir."

I send a quick text, and moments later, Jillian is back. I order salmon with sautéed green beans for both of us.

After Jillian leaves, I turn back to Angelina. "So tell me about your artwork."

A smile breaks out, and her eyes dance with excitement. For the first time today, she looks relaxed.

"I love to paint," she says, her face lighting up. "It's a release for me, a way to express myself when words fail me. It's like stepping into another world where all my troubles disappear, and I can just be. I don't know what I would do without it."

Her passion radiating off her stirs something profound within me. "I'd love to see more of your work if you wouldn't mind. I enjoyed the pieces I saw in your home."

"Really? I mean, of course, sir. It would honor me to show you."

We continued talking about her art, and I could see her eyes glimmering excitedly. As we wait for our food, I can't help but think about how much I want her. Something about her innocence and passion draws me in, and I know I must have her. Angelina is not like the women I used in Disorderly House. She is going to be my wife and will submit to my demands.

Our food comes, and I glance around the room. As I figured it would happen, the women of The Famiglia are stealing glances at Angelina. The few words I can lip-read have them wondering who she is.

"I can feel them staring. I'm sorry. I didn't mean to cause you any trouble."

"You didn't, Angelina. But we must do this now so they get used to it."

"What do you mean?" she asks.

"I have decided that I'm going to court you."

"What? Is courting like dating?"

"Yes and no. The Famiglia has rules for when a man courts a woman. It is how it has been done for centuries. The first step was me asking permission to begin the courtship from your father," I explain. It was a lie, but I didn't want her to know the truth. "The second step is for us to be seen in public. I plan on doing this a lot over the next few days."

I watch as she takes it in. "What is the next step?"

"Sorry, my dear, that is a secret," I say, wagging my eyebrows.

She sticks out her full bottom lip in a sexy little pout. Damn, my cock would love to have those pouty lips wrapped around him. "Pouting is naughty."

"I'm not naughty," she says.

"Oh, I think you are very naughty, and I can't wait until I see just how much."

"But I have never done anything before," she says, her eyes darting around the room before looking at me.

She looks at me with a mixture of curiosity and uncertainty. I give her hand a reassuring squeeze. "We can work things out together, Angelina. I'll ensure you're taken care of and that no harm comes to you. All you have to do is trust me."

"I do trust you, sir," she says, her voice barely above a whisper.

The rest of the meal passes in comfortable silence, with occasional glances between us. As we leave the restaurant, I can feel the eyes of the other patrons on us once again.

Once we are back in the car, I retake her hand.

"You did well in there. No one would ever know it was your first time at a restaurant."

"Thank you, sir."

"Angelina, when we are like this, you may call me Giovanni."

Her cheeks turn pink, and she lowers her head, her hair falling like a curtain blocking my view of her lovely face. I push back her silky locks so I can see her. "Angelina?"

"Okay, Giovanni," she whispers.

"Great. Now we have some shopping to do," I say.

"Shopping?" she asks.

"Yes. It is part of the courtship. I must prove to your father I can provide you with whatever you need."

"But I have everything I need."

"I am sure you do. However, I want you to dress in things only I pick out for you. From this day forward, I will supply every article of clothing you will wear."

"Why everything?" she asks.

"Because I am a dominant bastard who wants to know that those perky tits and sexy pussy are covered by things I purchased. If I can't touch them by my hand or mouth now, I love knowing the items I purchased are."

She shifts in her seat, and I see her chest jotting out a little. My little Angelina is turned on. Fuck, I bet I could make her come without even touching her. We pull up to the first boutique. Today was about getting the basics.

I had called earlier and had the shop closed except for two

sales clerks. The curtains were pulled, and shades were drawn down. No one would see Angelina except the sales clerks and myself. With the two female clerks as witnesses, it would keep the rules of The Famiglia intact.

As much as I want to fuck her into next week, it can't be done. I am bound by the rules, just as Angelina is. I can't have sex with her until our wedding night. Because of my station in The Famiglia, my first penetration must be witnessed by The Commission. Once I break through her virginity, I must withdraw and show the bloody proof to the members.

I've never been part of the ceremony since the other four founding sons are my age and unmarried. Yet my father told me details of the ceremony when I was fifteen.

I lean in and whisper in her ear. "If I could touch your nipples, I bet I would find them hard and your pussy wet with need. Am I right?"

Her creamy skin turns a deep pink. "Yes, sir," she moans. "Please touch me."

"I can't, and you won't either. Your purity must stay intact," I say. Then, a thought comes to mind. I gaze into her eyes. "Have you touched your pussy sexually?"

Her eyes grow wide, and her mouth hangs open. I can see how much of a shock my question was.

"No, Giovanni," she answers.

There was no sign of deceit in her eyes. I couldn't help but smile. I am a greedy bastard, and I want to be the one to give her first orgasm. I will take all her firsts and smile each time I do.

lay precariously close to the top. Her taunt nipples peeking over. Fuck me, they are perfect.

"Since the petals are in the back, I must pretend you have them. Hmm, I don't think you can see the placement if you have your bra on."

I reach around her, and the clasp comes undone with a flick of my wrist. Her heavy breasts tumble out. Damn, I can hardly wait to fuck these, but I won't be rushed when I do.

"Much better," I say as I fight myself not to touch. "You have to wear the petals because I don't want any asshole to see your hard nipples through the dress. They are mine. Now pretend you have the sticky pad and place it over your taunt nipple."

She looks down at her nipples and places her finger over the top of one. Her eyes close, and her mouth falls open. "Giovanni, please," she moans.

"What do you want?"

"I don't know. I feel it down there," she says as her eye drifts to her lap.

"You need to come. I can't touch your pussy because I don't think I could stop if I did. But I think I can make you come by playing with these. Place your fingers around the nipples and roll them back and forward."

"Oh, God, Giovanni, it feels so good." She bucks her hips up as she continues to play with her nipples.

Leaning forward, I allow myself to lick the tip of the hardened nipples before blowing on one, then the other. "Pull them hard, Angelina."

Without hesitation, she does, and her breaths pick up to where she is panting. I place my hand over the top of hers and pull them out further. This is not breaking the rules, but it is so very close. "Come for me," I command.

"GIOVANNI!" she screams as her body convulses. The bright pink hue colors her skin, and I know if I would rub my finger over her slit, she would be soaking wet.

She leans back against the seat, her eyes closed, gasping for breath. No one has ever looked as beautiful as she does at this moment.

She opens her eyes. The aquamarine orbits are hazy with lust. She brings her hand up and rubs my cheek. I lean forward and place a chase kiss on her lips. The car comes to a stop, and I pull back. Fuck, I lost track of time. I pick up her bra.

"Put this in your purse," I say. "And turn around so I can zip you up."

She turns, and I zip her up. After I finished, she stuffed the bra into her purse.

"You will tell no one what happened here," I instruct.

"I won't, Giovanni, but didn't your driver hear me screaming?" she asks.

"It is soundproof," I reassure her.

"Oh. I guess we better go before Daddy gets suspicious."

As much as I want to keep her here, I know she is right. I have broken one rule, but I will be careful not to let anyone find out. This wouldn't affect me, but her reputation would be in tatters.

"If we must. Stay put, and I will help you out. "

I open the door to find my security team surveying the area. Inside the estate, the walls should be safe, but I am not taking any chances.

Opening the door, I assist Angelina and wrap her hand around my arm. As we near the door, Charles opens it and smiles. He looks Angelina up and down. He lets out a deep breath as relief washes over him. Today, I focused on Angelina and how she handled being outside these walls. I never gave Charles one thought about how he was doing. For twenty-one years, he protected her, and suddenly, I'm removing her from the protective cocoon he had built.

Angelina looks up at me with a silent plea. I nod my head

and release her hand. She takes off and runs into her father's awaiting arms.

"Did you have a good time?" he asks.

"Oh, Daddy, I had such a great time. Lunch was delicious, and then Giovanni took me shopping."

"No problems?" he asks. I know he is asking about security issues.

"No, Charles. All was quiet."

"Good," he says as he squeezes Angelina.

"I have people coming to help her prepare for tonight," I tell Charles.

"You are going out again?" he asks.

"Yes," I say, my tone clipped. He knew once this started, I would see as much as I could of her until we were married. I need her to get comfortable with me so when I get down on one knee on Thursday, her expression will be genuine.

By his expression, he wants to say something, but he knows he can't. He set this in motion, and now he can only stand back and watch.

"I will be back at six, Angelina. Follow my instructions and be ready."

"Yes, Giovanni," she says.

I turn to walk back to the car. As I get close, I hear footsteps behind me. When I turn, I see Angelina.

"What is it?" I ask.

"I just wanted to thank you for a lovely lunch."

"You are very welcome. Now go rest. We have a big evening."

She looks up through her lashes and licks her lips. "I will, sir."

I couldn't help but chuckle. She definitely has a naughty side.

"See you in a few hours," I say and get in the car.

I watch as she walks back to her father, who instructs the staff to take in the shopping bags.

On the drive home, I mentally list what needs to be done. My house needs to be prepared for her arrival. The Genovese home hasn't had a mistress of the household for ten years.

My list is almost complete when we pull through the gate of the estate. I climb out and walk inside when we pull up in front of the mansion. Our long-time head housekeeper, Margaret, waits by the door as I walk in.

"Mr. Genovese, good afternoon," she says warmly.

"Good afternoon, Margaret. Please come to my office."

Her smile falls.

I place my hand on her shoulder. "It is nothing bad."

She follows me down the hall to my office. I sit behind the desk, and she sits in the chair across from me. "Margaret, I am getting married."

Her hand covers her mouth as she lets out a gasp.

"I know it is a shock. However, I need the manor prepared for her arrival."

"Certainly, sir. Whatever you want will be done," she says, straightening her back.

"I need the master suite cleaned from top to bottom. Ensure her closet is aired out and all the drawers, racks, and stands are in perfect working order. I want her sitting room cleared out of the old furniture. New furniture will be delivered on Friday. Also, the large room on the north side of the third floor cleared out as well. I want the walls painted a midlevel gray. My future wife is an artist, and this will be her studio. I'll install minimal equipment, but she will pick out the rest once she gets settled.

"When will the happy event happen?" she asks.

"Saturday."

"Oh, my."

"Yes. Also, I need everything prepared for the first night ritual."

She swallows and physically pales. She is well aware of the ritual since she was in the household when my father brought

enigmatic man who whisked me away from my mundane existence and into a world pulsating with excitement.

I close my eyes, allowing myself to get lost in the memories
of our encounters so far. His hands explored my body, leaving
a fire trail in their wake. Then, the intensity of his gaze as if
he could see straight into the depths of my soul. The
commanding authority in his voice sends shivers down my
spine. Giovanni awakened a side of me that I never knew
existed, a side that craved passion and danger in equal
measure.

As I lie there, anticipation simmering beneath my skin, I
can't help but wonder what tonight will bring. Our previous
encounters had been stolen moments, fleeting and full of
urgency.

Hazel finishes organizing the last of the clothes and
approaches me with a mischievous glint in her eyes. "Miss
Angelina," she murmurs. "Your young man has exquisite taste
in clothing. I don't think there is one piece that wouldn't make
you look like a queen."

I feel my face burn by her comment. It was the same thing
Giovanni said while I tried on the clothes.

I open my eyes, meeting Hazel's gaze. "Thank you," I
whisper, a mixture of nervousness and excitement coursing
through me. "I never imagined myself dressed like this, but it
all feels so...right."

Hazel's smile widens, her eyes sparkling with a secret
knowledge. "You were born to wear these clothes, Miss
Angelina. The way they will hug your curves and accentuate
your beauty...it's like they were made for you."

Her words awaken my newfound confidence. At this
moment, I am not just Angelina, the quiet artist hidden away
from the world. I am Angelina, the woman desired by
Giovanni and adorned in luxurious garments. The dichotomy
between my old life and this new one feels thrillingly intoxicating.

"All done," Hazel says, walking out of the closet. "Would you like me to start you a bath?"

The thought of soaking in a hot bath with loads of bubbles suddenly sounds incredibly enticing. "Yes, please," I reply, a hint of anticipation lacing my voice.

Hazel nods and disappears into the en suite bathroom. The sound of running water fills the room as she prepares the bath, adding fragrant oils and petals that will surely transport me to a realm of sensual bliss.

I take a moment to admire the opulent surroundings, the golden accents, and the intricate detailing that exudes timeless elegance. My father always made sure I had the best of everything.

As I slip off my clothes and step into the warm embrace of the bath, a sense of weightlessness envelops me. Closing my eyes, I lean against the porcelain tub, allowing my thoughts to drift towards Giovanni again.

The details of our lunch flash before my eyes, and I can't help but sigh. Every moment, he ensured that I felt safe and secure. The more time we sat in the restaurant enjoying our meal, the more relaxed I became. I spent my life behind the gates of my home, where I was safe from the monster who killed my brother and mother. But with Giovanni, an undeniable connection made me want to venture beyond those gates. He was like a beacon of light piercing through the darkness that had shrouded my existence for so long.

The image of his intense gaze, the way his hand brushed against mine as he poured me another glass of wine, lingers in my mind. I remember how effortlessly we fell into conversation, each word carrying weight and meaning. It was like we were two puzzle pieces, finally finding our perfect fit.

I dip my hand into the water, relishing in its warmth as it caresses my skin. The memories of Giovanni's touch flood my senses, igniting a fire within me that cannot be extinguished. With each passing moment, I can feel the anticipation building, the electricity in the air growing stronger. The thought of Giovanni's hands on my body, his lips tracing a path along my skin, sends a delicious shiver across my nerves.

And now, as steam rises from the bathwater and dances around me, I can't help but wonder what lies ahead. Will tonight be the night when everything changes? Will Giovanni show me a world beyond the confines of my fears? My mind begins to wander, imagining the possibilities that await me tonight. Will he whisk me away to a secret location where we can indulge our deepest desires? Or perhaps he has planned an intimate dinner at his opulent mansion, where we can bask in the glow of candlelight and surrender to the passion that simmers between us instead of a busy restaurant.

I close my eyes, allowing myself to be consumed by the heady daydreams that swirl within me. At this moment, time is suspended, and it is just me and him, two souls entwined in the intoxicating dance of desire.

Suddenly, my phone begins to ring. I knew it could be only one person, Giovanni. I pick it up, my hand covered in bubbles.

"Hello."

"Angelina." The gravelly growl of his voice ignites a primal desire within me, sending tingles racing from the crown of my head to the tips of my trembling toes. "I am proud of you for answering so promptly," he says, his words laced with an intoxicating mix of praise and possessiveness.

"Thank you, sir," I say with a smile. I know how much he loves when I call him that.

"All these brownie points you are earning will give you a delicious reward," he says.

My muscles tense, and my heart races as I contemplate the possibilities of what my reward might be, causing the warm water to slosh over the side of the tub. The steam rises in thick, billowing clouds, filling the room with a comforting humidity as I sink deeper into the fragrant bubbles. My mind swirls with anticipation, wondering what secrets and surprises await me at the end of this relaxing soak.

"What are you doing?" Giovanni asks.

"Taking a bubble bath."

"Fuck me," he moans.

I giggle. "I think that is against the rule."

"Among other things, but I like bending the rules," he chuckles.

"You are so bad," I giggle.

"Oh, Angelina, you have no idea. The hairdresser will be arriving soon. I just needed to hear your voice. Be a good girl, and I will think about giving you that award," he says and hangs up.

Moments later, there was a knock on my door. "Angelina, dear, the hairdresser is here for you," Hazel says.

I look past her to find a tall woman with dark, curly hair and a nice smile. "Hi, I am Lola. Mr. Genovese asked me to help you prepare for dinner tonight."

"Hi, Lola. I'm happy you are here to help."

The next hour, Lola styles my hair in a stylish updo. She helps me apply my makeup to make me look more sophisticated.

"Is there anything else you want me to help you with?" Lola asks.

"Can you help me get in my gown?" I ask.

"Sure, sweetie."

I stand and take the dress from the hanger. I turn my back, remove my robe, step into the gown, and pull it up, holding the top. Lola zips up the dress, and I turn.

"Oh, my stars, you are stunning," she says.

"Thank you," I say as I feel my face bloom with heat. I sit back on the bench and slip my feet into the stunning pink stilettos with pink feathers.

Slowly, I rise and turn towards the mirror. Who is this woman?

lustrous, while the diamonds glinted with every movement, just like her eyes. The delicate and intricate design mirrored her grace and poise.

"I'll take this set," I say.

"Wonderful choice, as always. I will put it on your account," Mr. Hinegard says with a broad smile. He places the velvet box in a bag and hands it to me. "If you need anything else, no matter the time, just call me."

"I will." Taking the bag I walk out of the shop. I caught my reflection in the window and wondered who this man was. I looked as if I was possessed, and I was possessed by her. She was everything I never knew I could have in one woman. I knew I had to be careful, that I had to keep my darker desires in check. I didn't want to scare her away, not after everything I had done to make her mine.

As I neared the vehicle, a black SUV passed by. I wouldn't think anything of it, but I was super hyper-sensitive with thoughts of the Cubans coming after Angelina.

I couldn't see anyone because of the dark windows.

"Did you see that, Hamm?"

"Yes, and I got the tag number. I will run it when we get back to the mansion."

"Put on an extra detail. I want them at the restaurant before we get there and then they can go to the theater. Make sure the men who follow us are aware of this situation."

"Yes, sir," Hamm says.

As soon as I rushed through the front door, my heart pounding in my chest, I knew something was wrong. Desperate for a release from the panic coursing through me, I stepped into the shower and let the scalding water beat down on my trembling body. How could the Cubans have found out about my relationship with Angelina? It had been over two decades since they last made contact with Charles, or so he thought. But now, as I stood there under the hot spray, I couldn't shake off the feeling that they had been watching him all this time, biding their time until they could strike again. Well, they picked the wrong man to mess with. With every ounce of determination in my body, I vowed to protect her at all costs. No matter what hell I had to unleash upon those who dared to threaten her safety.

These bastards know precisely how volatile I can be. Do they truly want to awaken Drago, the monster within me? The last time he emerged, I decimated an entire rival family's male population without a second thought. When I came back home, my entire body was drenched in their crimson blood, a haunting reminder of my uncontrollable rage.

On the drive to the Greco estate, I was on high alert. With every vehicle that came close to our car, I tried to get a look at who was in it. I saw nothing leading me to believe that the Cubans were in any of them.

Once my vehicle pulled through the gates of the Greco Estate, I sighed in relief. I wasn't sure it was the Cubans, and until I could prove it was them, I would keep it from Charles.

The housekeeper let me in with a warm smile, and I waited patiently for Angelina to make her grand entrance. I positioned myself to the side of the staircase, hidden from view at the top, eagerly anticipating the first glimpse of her. As soon as I heard the distinct click of her heels against the marble steps, I stepped out into view, and my heart began to race. She was like a dream, every bit as stunning as I remembered. My ears thumped along with my racing heart, their synchronized beats a testament to the overwhelming effect she had on me. With her graceful movements and alluring presence, she was truly a vision to behold.

I close the distance between us and take her hand. Bringing it up to my lips, I place a kiss on her knuckles, never taking my eyes off hers. "You look stunning."

A pink hue blooms across her face, which complements her gown. "You look very handsome as well."

"Thank you," I say, wrapping her arm around mine. I turn toward Charles. "We will be late coming back."

"Make sure she is safe," Charles says, worry evident on his features.

"With my life," I promise as I pull Angelina closer.

"Bye, Daddy," she says.

"Have a great time, sweetheart. I can't wait to hear all about it," Charles says.

I give him a nod and walk us out the door. Hamm opens the door, and I assist Angelina into the car. I get in, and Hamm pulls away. Once we are through the gate, I turn toward her."Did you bring the petals?"

A soft, delicate flush crept across her cheeks, spreading like a warm summer sunrise down her neck. Her fingers tremble as she reaches into her purse and retrieves the wrapped package. Without hesitation, she passes it to me and turns, offering her back for me to unzip her dress. When she faced me again, she sat with her hands folded neatly in her lap, a picture of grace and composure.

"My dirty little girl, you are learning so quickly," I praise. I pull down the front of the gown and let out a moan. I will never tire of looking at her perky nipples. I lean down and kiss each one. "We don't have time to play right now. However, if you are a good girl, maybe later. Now put them on."

She removes a petal from the package and places it over her puckered nipple. Damn it, it is so wrong to cover up such perfection, but no motherfucker was going to see them. They are for me and me alone. She covers the other one and pulls her dress back up. She turns, and I zip her dress. When she turns back, her mouth is turned down, and her eyes have lost their sparkle.

"What is wrong?" I asked.

"I just thought you might make me," she starts and bites her lip.

"Make you what?"

She lets out a deep sigh and fists her hands.

"Angelina, what do you want?" I ask.

"COME, GIOVANNI! I WANT TO COME!" she yells, eyes blazing with desire.

I chuckle. I have created an orgasm monster. "Angelina, you need to remember I am the one to give you orgasms or to deny them."

"But, Giovanni," she whines.

"No, little monster, no orgasms for you tonight. But I do have something for you," I say, picking up the black velvet box. "You pleased me earlier when you texted to ask what jewelry to wear. Did you not wear any because I didn't tell you what to wear?"

"Yes, sir."

"Perfect. I want you to wear these," I say, opening the box. Laying inside were the necklace and earrings I purchased for her.

"Oh my, they are stunning," she says, reaching out and running her finger against the pink diamonds. "Are these real?"

"Yes," I answer. Did she believe I would give her jewelry that wasn't the finest of quality? I take the necklace out and secure it around her delicate neck. Then, I attach the earrings to her small, soft ear lobes.

She raises her hand and rests it on the necklace. "Oh, Giovanni, thank you so much."

I take her hand and bring it to my mouth. I place a feather-light kiss on the back. "You are welcome."

Her full lips turn up into a radiant smile that outshines the fifty-five pink diamonds, one hundred-fifteen white diamonds, and the fifty pearls.

We just sit and stare at each other. I would never tire of looking at her.

So lost in her beauty, I didn't notice the car had stopped until I heard the tapping on the window. "Stay put," I instruct.

I step out of the vehicle and groan. Fuck me, the damn paparazzi are here. This was the first time Angelina would experience the assholes. My hand twitches to pull out my gun and take them all out. However, I didn't want Angelina to have to witness something like that.

With Hamm and Jessup flanking me on either side, we form a formidable barrier as we approach to Angelina's door. My hand hovers over the latch, my heart thudding in my chest like a war drum. As I pull open the door, my eyes meet Angelina's, her pupils dilated and darting frantically from side to side. The stench of fear and desperation seeps from every inch of her trembling body, making the air thick with tension.

"Angelina, you are okay. You will take my arm, and we will walk, our heads held high to the door. Don't look at any of them in the eyes and say nothing to them. I promise I will keep you safe."

"Okay," she whispers.

I take her hand, and she steps out with the grace of a queen. As soon as she emerges, the paparazzi goes crazy.

"Mr. Genovese, who is with you tonight?" one yells.

"Miss, what is your name?"

"Are you two dating?"

"Look over here."

I walk past the flashing cameras and into the entrance. When we get inside, I turn to face her. "Are you okay?"

"Yes, I am fine. I am just a little overwhelmed. Why do they care about who I am? I am nobody."

"You are not a nobody. You are Angelina Greco."

"But why are they so interested in me?"

"Because they haven't seen me out with a woman on my arm who wasn't my cousin. You are the first woman I've ever courted."

"First?" she gasps.

"Yes, first and the only one."

"Oh."

"Come, our table is ready," I say.

The hostess takes us to our table, which is, of course, the best.

All during dinner, conversation flows naturally between us. I was surprised by the amount of interests we shared. After a delicious meal, I paid the bill, and we were once again escorted out of the restaurant and to the car. We walked out the door, and I grit my teeth. The amount of paparazzi has doubled, hell, maybe tripled. I keep my arm protectively around Angelina. We are feet away from the car when a guy jumps in front of Angelina and begins taking pictures. She screams and hides her face in my chest. I see her body shaking as she grasps my jacket in a tight hold.

"GET THE FUCK OUT OF THE WAY!" I yell.

He didn't move.

"Giovanni," Angelina cries, trying to pull me even closer.

I give the fucker at least a two-second warning. I reach into my pocket and remove my gun. I aim it at his head. "Get out of the way, or I will take you out."

The Paparazzi's eyes grow large, and he steps out of the way. I usher Angelina into the back seat.

"Are you okay?"

She didn't answer. I place my hands on either side of her face. "Shh, I'm here."

"Why?" she asks.

"Why, what?"

"Why do you have a gun?"

I drop my hands. "Fuck, I forgot you have been sheltered all your life. Your father joined The Famiglia because he knew we could offer more security than he could. The Famiglia was founded centuries ago by five Italian families in Italy. Over the years, they brought others into the organization. The five families moved to the United States and settled in New York. The Bonanno, Gambino, Colombo, and Lucchese families split up the city in both criminal and legal enterprises. Those

give her a small smile, hoping to ease her nerves, before exiting the car and opening her door.

"Follow me," I say, holding out a hand to help her out of the car. She takes it hesitantly but doesn't pull away. We walk into the building together and take the elevator to the penthouse.

Once inside, I lead her to the living room and pour two glasses of bourbon. "Sit down," I say, gesturing to the plush couch. She sits down, and I take the seat opposite her.

She holds the glass, staring down at the amber liquid.

"Take a drink," I urge.

She lifts the glass and takes a drink. As soon as she swallows, she begins to cough.

I quickly move to her side, rubbing her back as she coughs. "Easy there," I say softly, taking the glass from her and setting it down on the coffee table. "You don't have to drink it if you don't want to."

She nods, still coughing a little. "I've never had hard liquor before," she says between coughs.

I chuckle softly. "It's an acquired taste," I say, sitting back down in my seat. "But let's get to why we're here."

I take a deep breath, trying to figure out where to start. "Angelina, I know finding out that I'm in the mafia was a shock. But I need you to understand that I'm not like the other men your father encountered. I don't hurt innocent people, and I would never hurt you."

She looks up at me, her eyes searching mine. "Then why are you in the mafia?" she asks quietly.

"It is my heritage. However, we are not like the movies that make us out to be. We must play our part to keep up the lie to the public. We get along with all the Italian families."

"What about the other families who are not Italian?" she asks.

"We fucking hate their guts. They are killers, especially the motherfucking Cubans," I growl.

"The ones who killed my mother and bother?" she asks with what I think is hope in her eyes.

I nod, my anger boiling just thinking about it. "Yes. They are responsible for what happened to your family."

Her eyes fill with tears once again. "Why would they do that?"

"Money, power, control," I spit out, my fists clenching. "They don't care who they hurt or kill to get what they want."

"I don't understand," she says, looking confused.

"I know," I say softly, reaching out to take her hand in mine. "But I promise you this, Angelina. I will make sure they pay for what they did to your family. They will suffer just like you and your father have."

She looks at me, her eyes wide. "How can you do that?"

"The Famiglia have connections," I say, a dark smile spreading across my face. "And they are not afraid to use them."

There is silence between us for a moment as she processes everything I just told her. "Will it bring them back?" she finally asks, her voice small.

I squeeze her hand gently. "No, it won't," I say, my heart aching for her. "But it will bring justice. And it will ensure that they can never hurt anyone else again."

She nods slowly, still processing everything. "Okay," she whispers.

I release her hand and stand up. "I know this is a lot to take in," I say, walking over to the bar and pouring myself another drink. "But I need you to understand that you are safe with me. I will never let anyone hurt you."

She looks up at me, her eyes full of a mix of fear and trust. "I believe you," she says quietly.

"Good," I say, taking a sip of my drink. "Because you're stuck with me now."

I can't help but feel a sense of relief as she smiles at me, a small glimmer of hope in her eyes. For a moment, I forget about the danger and darkness surrounding us. All I can focus on is her. Her eyes light up when she smiles, and her hair falls in soft waves around her face.

"I like that I am stuck with you," she says with one of her beautiful blushes. She bites her lip and looks out at the night. "I'm sorry to have ruined going to the play."

"Don't be. There are lots of them every night of the week in the city," I say with a smirk. I look at my watch and see how late it is. "As much as I wish we could stay here all night. I need to get you home."

Her face falls, and I think she feels the same as I do. "Okay."

I cup her face in my palm, and she leans closer. "Would you like to go on a picnic in the park with me tomorrow?"

"A picnic? Really? I've never been on one before," she says, her blue eyes dancing with excitement.

"I'll pick you up early, and we will take a walk around the park before we eat. So, let me get you home so you can get some rest."

We walked out of the apartment and to the elevator.

"Do you stay here a lot?" she asks.

"My offices are in the building, and it is nice to have some-where to crash when it gets late."

"Oh," she says as she shifts from one foot to the other.

"What is it you want to know?" I ask.

"Well, you said you haven't been seen out in public with women, and I wondered if you brought them here. I mean, you are a rich, good-looking guy, and I am sure you have needs."

"Are you asking me if I bring women here to fuck?" I ask.

She nods.

"Look, Angelina, you are very naive for a twenty-one-year-old. Have I had sex? Yes, lots of it. The Famiglia has a place where the members can go," I explain.

"So, are you still going to be with them even though we are courting?"

"No, Angelina. I will be faithful. However, you have to remember who the head of this relationship is. Your father said he explained how it is within The Famiglia."

"He did. I understand you are in control of everything, and I am sorry if I overstepped. I have never dated anyone before, but I don't think I could share you."

I wrap my arms around her and pull her close, feeling the warmth of her body against mine. She leans into me, and I can feel her heart beating in perfect rhythm with mine. "You don't have to worry about that," I whisper into her ear, my voice a gentle caress. She lets out a soft sigh as if all her worries are being carried away by the wind. Snuggling closer to my chest, she nestles herself in the crook of my arm. I breathe her in deeply, allowing her scent to envelop me in a warm sense of calm. It's like wrapping myself in a cozy blanket on a cold winter night, finding solace in her embrace.

We arrive in the basement and get into the car. During the entire ride to the Greco estate, I keep Angelina close to me, her head resting on my chest. The soft rise and fall of her breathing lulls me into a peaceful state. She falls asleep mere minutes into the drive, her petite form molds against mine as if we were made to fit together. Gazing down at her delicate features, I am struck by the weight of responsibility that now lies on my shoulders. She deserves to be happy and feel safe in this world, and I am determined to provide both for her. But as we approach our destination, doubts begin to creep in. Can I truly make her happy? Can I fill the void in her heart and bring a smile back to her lips? Or will my overpowering, controlling ways cause her to hate me? Only time will tell.

We pull through the gates of the Greco estate. I gently shake her awake. "We're here," I say softly.

She rubs the sleep from her eyes and looks around. "Oh, we are," she says groggily.

I help her out of the car and walk her to the front door. "I'll see you tomorrow for our picnic," I say, kissing her softly on the forehead.

"Thank you for tonight," she says, looking up at me with those beautiful blue eyes.

"Thank you for coming. Now, get some rest."

With that, I watch her walk inside before turning and heading back to my car. As we drive away, I can't help but think about her and the way she makes me feel. For the first time in a long time, I feel something. It is more than just lust or desire. It's a warmth that spreads through my chest, a sense of purpose I haven't felt in years. Angelina has awakened something in me, something I didn't even know was sleeping. And it fucking scares me.

I have always prided myself on controlling and keeping emotions at bay. But with her, it's different. She makes me vulnerable and strips away the walls I've built around myself. The thought of losing her, of failing to protect her, terrifies me more than any enemy I've ever faced.

What the hell was I doing? This was supposed to be a business arrangement, and here I was, all sweet and kind to her. I have never done any of those things in my entire life. I am the lord and master of my home, and she will be subservient to me in all things. Was I allowing her past to soften my feelings? She was unlike any other daughter within The Famiglia. When was the last time we had an adult daughter brought into the society? Hell, I can't remember. Normally, children of members are either born within the society or come in at a very young age. So when they grow up, they only know the rules of The Famiglia. Angelina has just become part of society and is being dropped into the deep end. She will have no time to prepare herself mentality for what is about to come.

As soon as I return to my estate, I go into my study to think. I bring over the bourbon decanter, pour a glass, and sit on my favorite leather high-back chair. Sitting there, I couldn't help but feel conflicted about the situation. On one hand, I knew I had to be firm with Angelina to assert my dominance and maintain order within The Famiglia. I couldn't let her get comfortable or think she could challenge my authority.

However, on the other hand, a part of me was drawn to her vulnerability and innocence.

I let out a frustrated sigh and took a sip of my bourbon. I need to figure out how to balance these conflicting emotions, or I risk losing control of the situation. I will talk with Angelina to lay out The Familia's expectations and rules and ensure she understands her place within it. Charles said he had explained it to her, but I want no doubt or misinterpretation of them.

Tomorrow, after we have our picnic, I will go over them again. No matter what she says, there is no going back at this point. I was going to do a grand proposal on Thursday. However, tomorrow may be better. I finish my drink and decide I need a few hours of rest. I climb the stairs and head to my bedroom. Walking in, I turn on the lights and see the subtle changes Margaret has made. A matching high-back chair with a soft-looking pink throw is sitting beside mine. Between the chairs is a new table with a Tiffany lamp. A crystal vase holds a fresh flower arrangement. My mother loved fresh flowers, and she had them throughout the house on a daily basis. I know Angelina will enjoy them, and I will have Margaret continue the tradition.

I walk into the closet, which will be Angelina's, and see Margaret has already cleaned it. She must have waited until I left this evening and started to work on it. I slip out of my clothes and head to the shower. The shelf of body wash and shampoo now contains several bottles of feminine products. I quickly shower and dry off. I climb into bed naked, and as soon as my head hits the pillow, I drift off to sleep.

What the fuck! I open my eyes to find I left the drapes open last night. I look at my clock to see it is six o'clock. Oh well, five hours is better than nothing. I get up, slip on my sleep pants, and head downstairs. Waiting at the bottom is Margaret with a cup of coffee.

"Good morning, Mr. Genovese," she says with one of her sweet smiles.

"Good morning, Margaret. I will be in my study for a little while before leaving for most of the day," I advise.

"Seeing Miss Angelina by chance?" she asks.

"Yes, and thank you for the touches you made to the bedroom. I know Angelina will love them." I give her a wink and walk to my study.

After taking a large drink of my coffee, I text Angelina, instructing her what to wear. Today was casual yet nice since we will be out in public. The lavender cap-sleeved dress I purchased yesterday would be a perfect combination of casual yet sophisticated. The white lace bra and thong were for my imagination only. My cock twitched at the thought of her wearing them. Down, boy, just a few more days until you can have your fill of her hot, wet pussy. I pull up my emails and see if anything needs to be handled. There is nothing pressing other than a few signatures on a couple of documents.

With a gentle knock on the door, Margaret entered, carrying a tray laden with a steaming carafe of coffee and a plate piled high with a perfectly folded egg white omelet and colorful fresh fruit. The aroma of freshly brewed coffee filled the room, mingling with the sweet fragrance of ripe berries and tangy citrus. I savored each bite, enjoying the burst of flavors in my mouth. As always, Margaret's cooking exceeded expectations. Suddenly, a thought struck me. Did Angelina have any specific dietary needs? Her health was something I took seriously, and it was my responsibility to ensure her well-being. I sent a message to Charles to find out if she had any issues with certain foods or other allergies.

I take a final sip of my steaming coffee, savoring the rich flavor before setting the cup down with a satisfying clink. My fingers quickly type out an email to the boutique, confirming our appointment later this afternoon. I can feel a knot forming in my stomach as I think about the conversation I have to have with Angelina. She needs to hear directly from me about the expectations for women within The Famiglia, and I know it won't be an easy conversation. However, she needed to know. Ignorance is not bliss in The Famiglia.

I go to my room and see the staff have already been in. The bed was made, and my suit from yesterday was put away. The dirt laundry was gone. The bathroom was spotless, with clean towels hanging on the warming rack. Turning on the shower heads and wait a few moments for the water to get to my preferred temperature before I strip and walk in. The hot water beats over my skin, and I allow it to release the tension in my shoulders. When I finish showering and shaving, I dress in black Armani slacks, a white button shirt, and a matching blazer. I won't wear a tie today to give the illusion of casualness. I could wear jeans or casual pants, but I am still the head of the family, and appearances still count. I place the Genovese family engagement ring in my jacket pocket and walk outside to find Hamm standing by the car.

"Everything arranged?" I ask, even though I know the answer would be yes. Hamm and my security staff were the best.

"Yes, sir. The teams have already done their sweeps and are stationed throughout the area. The picnic will be ready in front of Bethesda fountain at noon."

"Excellent."

I couldn't help but be a little nervous on the trip to Angelina's estate. By the end of the day, Angelina Greco will be my future wife with the Genovese engagement ring on her finger.

As we approach, I see her standing outside with Charles. Her radiant smile beams brighter than the sun above us. Her hair is neatly swept back into a low ponytail, and her face is adorned with just a hint of makeup, highlighting her natural beauty. She exudes an aura of freshness and wholesomeness that can only be described as pure and inviting.

She walks towards me as I exit the car. I take her hand in

mine and bring it to my lips. I kiss her knuckles, never taking my eyes off hers. She is stunning, and I am one lucky bastard. I pull her hand and place it around my arm. Glancing up, Charles gives me a respectful nod before returning to the house. Angelina looks up at me with those big, innocent eyes, and I feel a pang of guilt for what I know is coming later. But this is the way it has to be. For the sake of The Famiglia, for the sake of my reputation and status, I need a wife who will support me and uphold the values of our society. And Angelina is the perfect choice.

"Good morning, Giovanni," she murmurs.

"Good morning, Angelina. You look lovely today."

"Thank you. You look quite dashing yourself," she says with a smile.

I lead her to the car and hold the door open for her, sliding my hand down her back as she gets in. Once I am in the car, Hamm takes off.

We talk about trivial things. She behaves as if she is nervous about something. Could her nervousness be drawing off mine?

We finally arrive at the park and begin our stroll. Angelina looks around, her mouth slightly open as she takes in the sight. It was another first for her. "It is so beautiful," she says, grasping my hand.

Central Park is beautiful but didn't compare to her.

"Oh, look," she says, pointing to the horse and buggy. "Can we do that?"

I look over my shoulder at Hamm and nod. He takes out his phone to arrange it. It actually would be a perfect setting to propose.

We begin walking along the path, holding hands as Angelina takes in everything. My guard is a few yards ahead of us and in the rear of us.

Golden sunlight bathed the park, casting a warm glow over the bustling crowd. The air was heavy with the sweet fragrance of cherry blossoms and freshly mown grass. Despite it being a typical crowded weekend, the atmosphere was surprisingly serene. Families and friends lounged on picnic blankets, their voices blending into a symphony of laughter and conversation. Children darted through the fields, their joyful screams echoing through the trees. Amidst the chaos of the city, the park offered a peaceful oasis where one could escape into nature and forget about the outside world for a little while.

I ensure no one is around before I begin. "Angelina. Your father said he told you about the rules of The Famiglia."

"Ahh, yes, he did."

"Did he tell you that men are the heads of the household and what we say you must follow?"

"Yes."

"Do you understand your husband will have to be someone in the society?"

She hesitates for a moment. "I don't remember that."

I smile because she remembers my rule of lying. "You can't marry outside of The Famiglia. As a wife of a member of The Famiglia, you must obey him without question when it comes to sex. If he wants to tie you to the bed and fuck you until you pass out because of exhaustion, he has the right. If he wants you to crawl on your hands and knees, you will. He has the right to take you sexually anytime and anywhere."

She slows her steps, and I watch as she tries to understand my words. "But what about you? I don't understand. What do you like? Will you make me do those things?" she asks.

"I like to be in control and dominant. I like my woman to submit to me. I love fucking a woman until she is dripping with sweat and begging for mercy."

"Why?"

"It is part of who I am. Just because the wives submit doesn't mean they are not cared for. Their husbands will provide anything they need or want," I answer.

She is quiet again, trying to digest what I've told her or get the nerve to ask. I know she wants to know.

"My father loved my mother with all his heart. I can see it in his eyes when he looks at her picture or when he tells me stories about her. Giovanni, are there love in these marriages?"

"I can't answer that. My parents cared for each other. Father cared for her every need, and she, in turn, was obedient to him until her last breath. The marriages inside The Famiglia are arranged. Fathers align their positions to find a partner who will benefit the family. I don't believe in love, but it doesn't mean I won't care for my wife."

She slowly nods her head, her eyes fixated on the path ahead. A heavy silence hangs between us as she takes in all the information. My gaze is unyielding as I wait for her reaction.

I see the carriage ahead. Even though she is reeling from the information I gave her, we must move forward.

We walk up the carriage, and I stop us. "Angelina, your chariot awaits," I say in my best British accent.

Her eyes light up. The heaviest of our conversation falls away. "Really?" she asks, bouncing on her toes.

"Yes," I answer.

The coachman opens the door. "Welcome, miss. I hope you will enjoy your ride."

Angelina giggles as she climbs into the carriage. She snuggles back against the velvet cushions, smooths her dress, and pats the space beside her. I climb in and sit across from her, giving her the front view. I have seen all the sights but never seen them through her eyes.

Angelina's breath catches in her throat as the carriage begins to move. She eagerly scans her surroundings, trying to absorb every detail of the bustling streets. The vibrant colors and aromas fill her senses, overwhelming her with excitement and wonder. From the ornate architecture to the lively street performers, everything seems to come alive before her eyes. She can't help but gasp in amazement as the carriage continues on its path, each passing moment revealing more of the dazzling cityscape.

"Giovanni, look," she says, pointing to something.

I turn to see she is looking at the Belvedere Castle. Well, it is not a real castle. It's more of a picturesque castle built back in the 19th century. I have to admit, it's quite a spectacle to behold.

"That's the Belvedere Castle," I explain to her. "It's one of the most famous landmarks in the park. Built in the mid-1800s, it's a beautiful structure that serves as a popular spot for tourists and locals alike. It's said that it was constructed on a hill to offer a panoramic view of the entire park and the city beyond," I tell her, hoping to spark her interest in the beautiful sights around us.

"It looks so grand," she says, wide-eyed.

"It is, isn't it?" I reply, my own eyes tracing the intricate details of the structure. I can't wait until she sees the Genovese mansion.

"I always dreamed of living in a castle when I was a little girl," she says.

She will live in a castle. My family home is over 18,700 square feet with seven different levels. My great-great-grandfather built it when he migrated from Italy. Many of the original furniture is still in use today. As they say, good quality will last forever if you maintain it. Over time, we modernized the electrical, pumping, heating, and cooling but kept the original look and feel.

We are getting close to the end of the ride, and I know it is time for me to let her know she will be marrying me.

I slip my hand into my pocket and wrap my hand around the ring. I reach out and take her left hand.

"Angelina, you are beautiful not only on the outside but also on the inside. I promise to be patient until you learn your role. Just remember who the lord and master is over you," I say, slipping the ring onto her finger.

I stand up slowly, my mind racing with a million thoughts and emotions. But I know I have to play along, at least for now. I take his hand, my fingers trembling as I follow him out of the park and towards the high-end boutique.

As we enter the store, I am immediately overwhelmed by the opulence and glamour surrounding me. Rows and rows of designer gowns line the walls, each one more beautiful than the last. Giovanni leads me towards a rack of dresses. Each one with a color I would never wear, blood red. He picked out a few options for me to try on.

"Go change," he says, gesturing towards the dressing room. "I want to see how these look on you."

I nod silently, feeling like a doll being dressed up for display. As I try on each dress, Giovanni inspects me from head to toe, critiquing and commenting on every detail.

"This one is too plain," he says, tossing a dress aside. "This one is too revealing. This one is too frumpy."

I feel like I'm in a nightmare, trapped in a world where my worth is solely based on how I look and how well I please my fiancé.

Finally, he hands me a dress that he approves of. It's a red satin gown with Swarovski crystals in a design of flames, with a plunging neckline and a slit up the side. He tells me to put it on, and I obey, feeling like a puppet on strings.

When I step out of the dressing room, Giovanni's eyes light up with approval. "Yes, this is perfect," he says, running his hand down my arm possessively. "You look beautiful, Angelina."

I want to scream, rip the dress off me, and run out of the store. But I know there's no escape, not yet.

Just as I think we are finally leaving, the sales clerk brings in a different rack. This time, it is wedding gowns. All pure white and modest. Unlike the red dress he chose for the ball, these dresses would cover everything. Was there a reason for this?

Giovanni's eyes light up at the sight of the white gowns, his fingers tracing over the fabric with a possessive touch. "These are the ones," he says firmly. "No need for anything too revealing at the wedding. You will be the perfect little virginal bride."

My heart sinks as I realize that even my wedding dress is not my choice. Giovanni picks a few options for me to try on, each one more modest and traditional than the last. I try to protest, telling him I want something that feels like me, but he silences me sternly.

"Try them on, Angelina," he commands. "I want to see which one looks the best on you."

Feeling defeated, I retreat to the dressing room and try on the dresses. They are all beautiful in their own way, but none feel like me. They all feel like costumes, like I'm playing a role in someone else's story.

I step out of the dressing room in the last dress, and Giovanni smiles. But this time, his gaze is different. It's not possessive or controlling but almost...admiring.

"That one," he says softly, his fingers tracing over the lace and satin of the dress. "That's the one you'll wear when you become my wife."

For a moment, I forget all the reasons why I hate him, why I'm terrified of him. I forget about the red dress and the ball and the fact that I am now the property of a powerful mafia family and The Famiglia.

All I see is the way he's looking at me, the way he's making me feel. And even though I hate myself for it, I feel something flutter in my chest.

Maybe there's a chance that I can turn this situation around. I can use his feelings for me to my advantage, to gain some measure of control or maybe even freedom.

But then Giovanni's expression hardens, and the moment is shattered. "Come, we have much to do before the wedding," he says, taking my hand and leading me out of the store.

As soon as we walk out, the front of the store is packed with paparazzi. His security guards are holding them back. I can feel the weight of their invasive presence as they snap photos and shout questions at Giovanni and me. The flash of cameras blinds me momentarily, but Giovanni's grip on my hand remains firm and unyielding.

"Mr. Genovese, is it true you are getting married?" one of the reporters shouts out.

All the other times, we walk straight to the vehicle without paying them any attention. But Giovanni stops and wraps his arm around my waist. He leans down to my ear.

"Put your left hand on my chest."

When I don't do it, he squeezes my waist and gives me a look that I would regret it if I didn't comply.

I hesitantly place my left hand on his chest, and I feel the steady thump of his heartbeat reverberating beneath my palm. Giovanni's voice echoes loudly and clearly above the clamor of the paparazzi, commanding attention with its smooth timbre. The flashing lights and shouting voices fade into the background as I focus on his firm chest, rising and falling with each breath.

"Yes, it is true," he says, his eyes never leaving mine. "Angelina here will be my wife."

The reporters go wild, shouting questions and trying to get closer to us. But Giovanni's security team keeps them at bay, forming a protective circle around us.

Giovanni leans in closer to me, his lips brushing against my ear. "Play along, Angelina," he whispers. "Let them believe that we're in love."

I smile up at him, trying to look as besotted as possible. He does the same, though I know it is a lie. He leans down and places a quick, soft kiss on my lips. When he pulls away, he gives me a wink and starts walking toward the car.

We finally make it to the vehicle, and once inside, I sit still with my head lowered and my hands on my lap. I didn't want to anger him any more. I just want to go home and have a good cry in my bed.

"Angelina, I will allow you to pout today, but no more. Tomorrow we will go out to lunch with your father. You will smile and act like you are head over heels in love with me."

Tears burn my eyes. "What happened to the man who took me lunch? The man who held me when I found out you were in the mafia? I know I wasn't imagining it. You were tender and loving."

"I am sorry I confused you, but this is the real me. You will be Angelina Genovese, royalty within The Famiglia."

"I don't want to be royalty. I just want to have a loving relationship with my husband."

"You will be royalty, and as long as you are submissive and obedient to me, we will have a happy marriage. But if you disobey me or try to run away, I will make sure you regret it." The threat in his voice sends shivers down my spine.

I know I'm in too deep now and can't just walk away from this. But maybe, just maybe, I can find a way to survive. Perhaps I can find a way to make him love me and see me as more than just a doll to be dressed up for display.

As I sit there, staring out the window at the passing cityscape, I vow to do whatever it takes to find a way out, even if it means playing with Giovanni's twisted game for a little longer.

We finally make it back to my home. As soon as the car stops, I reach for the handle. I want out of the car and away from him, even if it's just until tomorrow.

His hand clamps down on my leg and squeezes. "Don't even think about it. You stay there and wait for me to help you out."

I look up at him and shudder at the darkness I see in his eyes. Why hadn't I seen it before?

Doing as he says, I sit and wait until he opens the door. He wraps my hand over his arm and walks us to the door. As we near, Daddy walks out.

"Hey, did you have a good time," he says.

"We had a wonderful time, Charles. Angelina and I are engaged," Giovanni says with a smile.

Daddy rushes forward and pulls me into a tight hug. "Congratulations, baby girl."

I know my little fiancée is not happy. She thinks I can't read her thoughts, but she doesn't know about my abilities. She is badly mistaken if she thinks she can run away from me.

"Angelina, why don't you rest and then pack your room," I say.

She wrenches herself away from her father's embrace and locks eyes with me, her expression filled with a fiery determination. The demure, submissive facade crumbles in an instant, revealing a fierce and unyielding spirit within her. A wicked smirk spreads across my face as I realize the challenge she presents to me. The thought of breaking her down, making her surrender to my will, sends a thrill through my body. I can't wait to claim her completely in bed after she puts up a deliciously defiant fight.

"I can do it tomorrow," she says through gritted teeth.

"You have appointments tomorrow."

"What appointments?" she growls.

I raise an eyebrow. "Angelina, come over here."

Her eyes narrow into razor-sharp slits as she stands unwaveringly by her father's side, a glimmer of determination in her gaze. Did she genuinely believe he would shield her from me?

"Charles, Angelina, and I need to have a little talk. I will be taking her to your study," I say, not asking for his permission. Before she can even blink, I move and grasp her elbow. I escort her into the house, down the hallway, and into Charles's study, but I don't shut the door.

"Angelina, I have warned you several times what would happen if you didn't listen to me."

She tries to wrestle out of my gasp. "LET GO OF ME!" she screams.

I eye a chair without arms. I sit down in the chair and pull her in front of me. "I can't say I didn't hope you would make me do this because I have dreamed of turning your milky white ass red."

Her mouth falls open. "You can't do that."

With a lightning-quick movement, she is draped over my legs, and her dress rides up to her waist in a flash. She thrashes wildly against me, bucking and kicking with all her strength. I deliver a sharp spank to her exposed backside, eliciting a blood-curdling scream from her lips. "Your futile struggles only fuel the intensity of your punishment," I growl through gritted teeth. "If you persist, it won't be just my hand but my leather belt that will leave its mark on you."

Her body tenses and every muscle coils like a spring as she finally realizes there is no escaping this, no changing my mind. I can see the fear and desperation in her eyes as she surrenders to my will.

I grip the thin fabric of her panties in my fist and yank them down, exposing her flawless ass. It's like a work of art, smooth, creamy skin without a single flaw or imperfection. My hand glides over her perfectly rounded globes, eliciting a soft moan from her lips. But as my fingers inch closer to her core, she instinctively clamps her thighs together, denying me access. In response, I deliver a sharp slap to the top of her thighs, demanding compliance. "Spread your legs," I growl, my voice filled with authority and desire.

"NO!" she yells.

"Do I have to bring in Hamm to help me hold them apart?"

"You wouldn't dare?" she growls.

"Hamm," I say.

"Yes, Mr. Genovese," he answers from the doorway. He won't come in unless I tell him, but Angelina doesn't know this. She tries to cover her ass with her hands, but I grasp them with one hand, holding them to her lower back.

"Do that again, and I will tie them," I say.

"Please, don't," she cries. "I'll be good."

I smile. "Hamm, wait outside the door."

"Yes, sir," he says.

I wait a few moments before I say anything. "Angelina, you are being punished because you were disrespectful. You also screamed at me and tried to run. For these offenses, you will get twenty punishment spanks."

"TWENTY!" she yells.

"Do you want it to be twenty-five? Because every time you yell, I'll add five more. You try to cover your ass, I add five, you close your thighs, I add five. Do you understand?"

"Yes," she says.

I slap her hard, causing her to jump. "Yes, what?"

I wait, just as I am about to give her another spank. "Yes, sir."

"Better. I will start with ten warm-up spanks. Don't want to bruise your tender bottom too badly."

With each resounding smack, I can feel her body tense up in resistance. Her struggles only fuel my determination as I continue to deliver powerful spanks, each one more forceful than the last. She fights back with all her might, but I know by the end, she will succumb to me completely, broken and submissive under my control.

"Alright. I want you to count each one and thank me. If you don't, I'll add five more," I instruct.

"Giovanni," she says, her voice breaking. "Can you please close the door?"

"No. I don't care who hears."

"My father," she whispers. "Will hear."

"Probably, but as your future husband, I am in control, not him."

She lets out a sigh.

"Alright, let's begin." I swing my arm and land the strongest spank so far.

"Ow," she cries.

"Angelina?"

"One, thank you, sir," she rushes out.

I continue to increase the strength with each one. When I reach ten, she is crying. I rub my hand over her red heated ass and then rub my finger between her legs. I still my raging hard-on as I feel her slick lips. Fuck me, she is drenched. My little shy bride-to-be is turned on by me spanking her. Good, because I love giving pain while a fuck. I dip my finger inside, and she moans. Shit, it is tight, and the thought of me being the only one to ever be inside her makes me want to throw her on the floor and sink my dick deep.

"Hmm, you might scream and cry, but you can't deny your punishment turns you on. This is a punishment spanking, so no release for you."

"Please," she groans, clamping down on my finger.

I remove my finger and return to her punishment. The next ten are the worst. I put all my power behind each one, and she thanked me as I landed the last one. Then she collapses. Her lifeless body hangs over my legs.

I quickly turn her, and she begins to shake uncontrollably. Fuck, she is dropping out of what is called subspace.

"Angelina? Angelina, wake up," I say, shaking her.

She opens her eyes, and I cup her face in my hands. "You did good. Do you want to stay here or go to bed?"

She places her hands over my wrists. "Bed."

I scoop her up in my arms, wrap a cover which is on the back of the couch, and walk out of the office. Hamm lowers his eyes as we walk past him.

Charles looks at me and then at Angelina. Concern was written all over his face. He goes to say something, and I shake my head. I pull her closer, making sure her face is buried into my chest. I carry her up the stairs and to her room. I lay her on the bed and remove her dress, leaving her only in her bra. Fuck, I can't have that. I reach around and unclasp it, causing her heavy breasts to fall. I bit my lip and climb in beside her. I pull the blankets over us, and she curls up to me.

I am still aroused from spanking and playing with her. I gently rub her ass, and she whimpers. Fuck she is so sexy, even in pain, and she is mine. I bury my face in her hair and inhale her scent. I gently kiss her neck, and she leans her head to the side, giving me more access. I lick her skin, and she sighs and turns her head. I continue to lick her neck and nip at her.

"I am proud of how you accept your punishment. Next time, I won't be as gentle."

"Next time?" she asks, her voice cracking.

"Baby, I have a feeling you are going to be over my lap or my whipping bench a lot."

She shakes her head. "Nope, I am going to be good."

I chuckle and pull her closer. We lay like this for a while. She sighs and soon falls asleep. I hold her a little longer before easing out and leaving the bed. I make sure she is covered up before going into the bathroom. I open the drawer and find a tube of cream. Going back into her room, I pull back the covers and examine her ass. It is red, and my handprint can be seen, but it shouldn't bruise. I apply a generous amount of cream and rub it onto the heated skin. She lets out a moan but doesn't wake. When I am satisfied, I cover her back up. I wash my hands and leave her room, closing the door behind me.

When I reach the bottom of the stairs, Charles is waiting for me.

"She is fine."

"Wasn't that a little extreme?" he asks.

"No. She must learn. When she awakes, don't coddle her. I am having boxes being delivered for both her possessions and her artwork. The movers will be here tomorrow."

"She is moving in tomorrow?" he asks.

"No, but I want everything set up when we return from the wedding," I answer.

"You said she is busy Friday. Is there something I am supposed to do?"

"No," I say and look around. I took a step closer, ensuring he was the only one going to hear this. "The Famiglia requires a test before a woman marries a member."

"What type of test?" he asks.

I raise my eyebrow. "Charles, don't make me say it. You are a smart man, and I am sure you can figure it out."

I watch his face as he tries to figure it and I can tell the second he does. He shuts his eyes and shakes his head.

"Charles, I promise I will make it as painless as possible, but The Famiglia doctor must certify it."

"Will you be in the room?" he asks.

"No. I am not allowed to be in the room. My second will be to ensure the procedure is certified to my standard as well. I have already spoken to him, and he knows my rules while he is in the room."

"I still have much to learn about the society," Charles admits.

"You do, and to be honest, Charles, I recommend you not to read about the ceremonies which follow the wedding. Just know I will do everything I can to ensure she is protected."

"Thank you, Giovanni. I know this wasn't something you

wanted initially, but I know in my heart you are the man who will always protect her."

"I will, and even though it might seem cruel, I do it for her own good when I discipline her," I say, then remember I forgot something in his office. "Charles, I left something in your office."

I walk back to his office and find Angelina's lavender panties where I had dropped them. I pick them up and stuff them in my pocket. Later in my bed, I will use them to give my cock some relief.

I have a lot of details I must line up for not only the ball but our wedding. We are back in the car, and as we pull out of the estate, I notice a few cars and vans. Well, I guess the fucking sharks have figured out who Angelina is.

"Hamm, did you see that?" I ask.

"Yes, sir."

"Have two additional security teams here ASAP. They are to work with the Greco security team," I instruct. "Also, make sure Charles is advised of the situation."

"Will do. Where to now?"

"The compound. I need to advise The Commission of my intention to marry."

Hamm and my security begin our drive to The Famiglia compound. I take out my phone and text the other four founding sons and the four consigliere. They will arrive at the compound within the next hour. When a founding son asks for a meeting, they will drop whatever they are doing and come. They know, as I do, that founding sons only ask for a meeting if it is important.

Chapter Fourteen

GIOVANNI

My car pulls up the tall black iron gates of The Famiglia Compound. When I called for a council meeting, I forgot how I dressed. Thankfully, we passed the Genovese estate on the way, and I rushed in and changed into one of my best suits. It is not every day a man announces his engagement to The Commission. Fuck, that reminds me I need to call my father and let him know before he gets a call from one member congratulating him.

My father, Raphael Giovanni, was still a prominent member of The Famiglia. Even though he is retired, he is still very active in The Famiglia in our Italian branch. He is a founding son and serves on The Commission in Rome as the representative of the Genovese family.

There are three Commissions in The Famiglia. One is in New York, one is in Rome, and the third is in Brazil. Each one has a blood relative to the first five families and four elected consigliere sitting on The Commission. My uncle served on the Brazilian commission until his death. Now, my second cousin serves. Robert is my grandfather's brother's grandson. Each is tasked with the governing members of The Famiglia.

My car stops at the gate, and Hamm swipes my ID card.

The heavy iron gate, adorned with intricate designs of the five founding family animals, swings open with a resounding creak. The massive dragon's wing, spanning the width of the gate, embraced a proud raven on the right and a fierce lion on the left. Its long tail curls protectively around a mighty bear and a cunning wolf, symbolizing the family's unwavering protection of all its members. The detailed engravings on the gate glint in the sunlight, telling stories of ancient battles and triumphs. As it opens, a sense of pride and history washes over those who enter through its threshold.

The Famiglia compounds are the epitome of security, impenetrable fortresses designed to protect those within. Surrounded on all sides by an imposing eight-foot stone wall, their strength and invincibility are immediately apparent. Each inch of the wall is covered in state-of-the-art motion detection sensors and cameras, giving a sense of constant vigilance and watchfulness. As members of The Famiglia, we have access to the most advanced security systems available, setting us apart from any other place in the world. Only the two other compounds can rival our level of protection and sophistication.

Beyond the towering walls lay a sprawling complex of buildings. The central structure holds the grand ballroom and the administrative offices. The building has a well-equipped industrial kitchen and pantry that stood ready to efficiently serve up to five hundred guests at a moment's notice. On the left side of the main building, essential facilities such as security, an armory, a gym, and a clinic could be found. The imposing judicial building, Palazzaccio, houses The Commission chambers looms to the right, its halls echoing with the weight of justice. This was where members who dared to break the rules were brought to face The Commission's judgment and receive their punishment. The air inside the compound was heavy with authority and power, a tangible reminder of the organization's control over its members.

The car glides to a stop in front of the entrance, and a sharply dressed staff member emerges to open my door. He is dressed head-to-toe in a impeccably tailored black suit, shirt, and tie. Not a hair is out of place on his short-cropped hairstyles, and there is no trace of facial hair. His appearance is how every male staff member is required to look. The female staff members are equally polished in their elegant black dresses, sheer stockings, and high heels. Their glossy hair is pulled back into neat buns, with only a touch of makeup allowed to adorn their faces. Jewelry is limited to a simple, understated gold wedding band. These staff members are here to serve us with utmost professionalism and discretion, blending seamlessly into the background when not attending to their duties.

"Good day, Mr. Genovese," he says.

I nod and head toward the door, where another staff member opens it.

"Good day, Mr. Genovese."

"Thank you," I say. I walk through the maze of hallways until I reach the double wood doors engraved with a similar image as the front gates. I straighten my tie and pull my shirt cuffs out from my jacket. Turning the knob, I open the door and walk in and see the rest of the commission are seated around the grand oak table.

"Viva la Famiglia Unita," I pledge as I take my spot at the table.

"Viva La," they all say.

"Thank you all for coming on short notice," I begin. "I wanted to inform you I have selected the woman who will become my wife."

Their faces twist into expressions of shock and disbelief, except for Davide, who wears a knowing smirk. I was the first of the founding sons on this commission to become engaged.

"Congratulations, Giovanni," Consigliere Morgan says. "And who is the lucky woman?"

"Angelina Greco," I say as I look at each of them. All look surprised. However, Consigliere Morgan's expression has an undertone of something else. Was it disdain or hatred?

I couldn't tell, but I made a mental note to monitor him. The Commission is quiet for several minutes before Davide speaks up.

"Well, I think this calls for a drink," he announces before going to the cabinet. Opening the door, he pulls out one of the five special bottles of bourbon. The bottles were purchased on the day of our births and stored until this day.

Davide pours the bourbon into glasses. I scan the faces around the table. Everyone, except for Peter, seems genuinely happy for me. Even the usually stoic Robert has a smile on his face.

I take a slow, deliberate sip of the bourbon, relishing in its smooth warmth as it cascades down my throat. The rich amber liquid dances on my tastebuds, leaving behind notes of oak and caramel. With a satisfied sigh, I set the glass back in the leather chair and look at the worn wooden table, admiring how the light catches the delicate etchings on its surface.

"Thank you, everyone. You will meet her tomorrow evening at the Fire and Brimstone ball. We will announce our engagement during the event," I say.

"When is the wedding?" Peter asks.

"Saturday evening," I answer.

"So soon?" Peter asks. "You know a virginity test has to be conducted before the wedding. I can call Doctor Garner and attend the test as he performs it."

I grit my teeth. There would be no way in hell I would allow him in the room when Angelina is given the virginity test. And Doctor Garner wasn't going to perform the test. Several times, I came upon him at events where he was making inappropriate remarks about women he had examined. Most of the doctors of The Famiglia are males, but we also had several female doctors on staff who made our females more comfortable. I will have Dr. Bianchi do the test. She has done several tests and treats the woman with the utmost care and consideration.

"I have asked Dr. Bianchi to perform the test and have selected my second."

Peter's eyes narrowed. "Who? Because it has to be someone on The Commission."

"That would be me," Davide says, giving me a wink.

Peter looks between Davide and me, trying to figure out when I had asked. His eyebrows furrow and his mouth tightens. "Giovanni, I don't believe Angelina Greco is high enough in the echelon for your station."

I raise an eyebrow at Consigliere Morgan. "What do you mean?" I ask, trying to keep my voice calm.

"Well, she's not from one of the first five families, is she?" he says, his tone condescending.

I can feel the anger boiling inside of me. How dare he question my choice of partner? But I remain calm and take another sip of bourbon before responding.

"No, she's not," I say firmly. "But she comes from a respectable family and is everything I want in a wife."

Consigliere Morgan snorts. "I think it's a mistake. The Famiglia needs to maintain its traditions and standards."

The air in the room weighs heavy, charged with a palpable tension that threatens to explode at any moment. I can feel my heart pounding in my chest as I scramble to find a way to calm the rising storm before it unleashes its full fury. Drago wants out, and his sights are set on Peter.

"I understand your concerns, Consigliere Morgan, but I assure you that Angelina will make an excellent addition to The Famiglia," I say.

The rest of the commission nods in agreement, and Consigliere Morgan reluctantly backs down. The meeting continues smoothly, but I can't shake off the unease that

Consigliere Morgan's words had left me with. I will keep a close eye on him in the future.

Everyone leaves except Davide and I as we sit and finish up the bottle.

Davide leans toward me. "What the fuck is up with Consigliere Morgan?"

"I don't know, but he almost left here with missing teeth," I grit out.

"I'll keep an eye on him," Davide says.

"Thank you, and I'm going to do an investigation on him as well."

"Giovanni, you have to be careful when investigating a consigliere. You can't do it without merit," Davide says.

"I know, but I have a bad feeling about him," I say, leaning back in my chair. "I need to make sure he won't cause any problems."

"I agree, but you have to be cautious," Davide warns. "He's an old-school traditionalist. He doesn't like change or anything that goes against the rules."

"I'll keep that in mind," I say, finishing off my glass of bourbon. "But for now, let's focus on the engagement and the wedding. I want everything to go smoothly. Can you come to lunch with us tomorrow? I want Angelina to get to know you before the test."

Davide nods before standing up. "Sure thing. Where are you going?"

"Tavern on the Green at twelve-thirty," I say, pouring the last of the bourbon into our glasses. "Thank you for being my second."

"Sure thing, brother, and maybe in the distant future, you can repay the favor," he says with a smirk.

"I won't be holding my breath on that one." Davide has demons concerning marriage. The men in his family for generations openly fucked around on their wives.

As I sip the bourbon, I can't help but think about

Consigliere Morgan's words. He's right. Angelina doesn't come from one of the founding five families, but I don't care. She's the only woman I want to marry. And if anyone tries to stand in our way, they will have to face the consequences.

I finish the last of the bourbon and head out of The Commission chambers. The staff member opens the door for me, and I nod in appreciation before heading to my car. Hamm drives me home. My mind is consumed with thoughts of Angelina and our future together. But in the back of my mind, I can't shake off the feeling that someone is watching me, waiting for a chance to strike.

When I arrive at my estate, I head to my bedroom for a shower. After washing away the day, I crawl into my bed naked. As I close my eyes, I can feel the day's events catching up with me, and I soon drift off to sleep.

My mind becomes a battlefield as I am tormented by haunting visions of Consigliere Morgan's scathing sneer. My body jolts awake in a clammy, cold sweat, my heart hammering against my chest. The weight of my marriage to Angelina is crushed by the burden of caution, knowing that I must be careful but unable to let anyone come between us and our happiness.

I get out of bed, slip on sleep pants, and head to my office. I have work to do. I need to make sure everything is perfect for the engagement and wedding. I spend the rest of the night reviewing every detail, ensuring everything is in order.

As the sun begins to rise, I know it's time for me to get some rest. I head back to my bedroom, hoping the nightmares won't return. But as I lay in bed, I couldn't help but wonder what Consigliere Morgan was planning and how I could stop him. I close my eyes and try to push the thoughts from my mind, knowing I need rest.

My alarm goes off, and I want nothing more than to stay in bed. However, I have lunch with Angelina and Charles.

Hamm screeches to a halt in front of the sprawling Greco

estate, and my heart jumps into my throat as I see Charles standing on the steps. His face is twisted with fear and dread. Without a second thought, I bolt out of the car and sprint toward him."

What is wrong?" I ask, my heart racing.

He looks over his shoulder and then back at me. "I received an email this morning."

"From who?" I ask.

"I don't know, but whomever it was knew all about Cecila and Jimmy's death. It said if I didn't stop this wedding, Angelina would be next," Charles says. The fear in his eyes was painful to see.

My heart sinks at Charles' words. This is precisely what I feared. Someone is trying to stop our union, and they're willing to go to extreme lengths to do so.

"I promise you, I will stop at nothing to protect her."

"I know. It just brought up all those old feelings. I've kept her hidden all her life, and just when she begins to have a normal existence, this happens. Do you think it is Maeto?"

I know he should be the first person it should be. However, my gut is telling me it is not Maeto. "Charles, I don't know, but I will not stop until I get an answer," I say. "How is she this morning?"

"Quiet. She asked if you called me at breakfast," he says.

Fuck, fuck, fuck. I should have called or texted her this morning. After last night, I was sure she was conflicted. "I'm sorry I didn't. I had a long night and didn't fall asleep until the sun rose. Is she ready for lunch?"

"No. She is in her room waiting for you to tell her what to wear. I told her you must have been busy and just to put something on, but she refused."

I had instructed her that I had complete control over every aspect of her life. But only a few days later, I fumbled and let the ball drop. Despite my mistake, there is no denying that she is the perfect match for me. Every fiber of my being is drawn to her, like a moth to a flame. In her presence, I feel both powerful and vulnerable simultaneously. It's a feeling unlike any other, one that leaves me craving more. And in this moment, I know that she is the missing puzzle piece in my carefully constructed life.

Chapter Fifteen

GIOVANNI

I stand at the fork in the hall, unsure of which path to take. Part of me wanted to follow Charles and try to unravel the mystery of the email, but another part longed to go upstairs and see Angelina. My heart beat like a thundering heart as I tried to decide, but ultimately, I knew the choice I had to make.

"Hamm, go with Charles and let him show you the email?" I instruct and head inside.

Bounding up the stairs, my heart racing with anticipation, and I reach her room in record time. Pushing open the door, I am greeted by an almost unnatural darkness. The only light source is the sun's glow filtering through the windows. My eyes search the room, taking in every detail. Where could she be? And then I see her perched on a plush bench near the window. She is clad in one of the luxurious satin robes I gifted her, her knees tucked tightly against her chest. Her slender fingers clutched her cell phone, her attention fully absorbed by its screen. Despite her stillness, I can sense a storm of emotions brewing within her. It beckons me closer, drawing me to her side as if pulled by some invisible force.

"Angelina," I call out.

She doesn't respond, her attention consumed by the cell phone in her hand. She looks at the screen and lets out a heavy sigh, I can sense the storm brewing inside her. When she doesn't see what she wants to see on the screen, she pulls her knees to her chest, her hair falling forward like a curtain of protection around her face. Damn it, why do I have to follow the rules? I should have stayed with her last night, no matter what. The rush of endorphins from our intense session of spanking was unlike anything she had ever experienced before. But now that it's over, she crashes hard as they wear off, leaving her emotionally drained and vulnerable.

I walk over to her and sit on the other end of the bench. My heart aches to see her like this, knowing it was my fault.

"Angelina," I say.

She doesn't look at me but shakes her head.

"What is wrong?" I ask even though I know. I need her to start talking.

"He hasn't texted me?" she sniffles.

"Who?" I ask.

"Padrone del mio cuore, corpo e anima," she answers.

My heart skipped a beat hearing this in our native language. She declares the statement with such convection. It is the same statement she will recite at the ceremony in front of the council. Master of her heart, body, and soul.

I need to think of a way to make her acknowledge me to break her from this trance she is under. She rechecks the cell phone once again. It hit me. I take out my phone and text her, hoping this would snap her out of it.

Her phone chimes, and she jumps. A smile breaks across her face, and she puts the phone against her chest. She looks up and gasps. "Giovanni?"

A grin spreads across my face as I outstretch my arms, inviting her into my embrace. Without hesitation, she leaps into my waiting arms and wraps herself around my neck in a loving hug. The warmth of her body and the scent of her perfume fills me with a sense of comfort and joy. In this moment, nothing else in the world matters except for the two of us, locked in an embrace that speaks volumes without a single word spoken.

"You are here," she mumbles.

I rub my hand up and down her back over her robe. She is naked underneath I have to see and feel all of her.

"I need to feel you," I say as I pull back. Her eyes meet mine, and I see she needs it as well. She unties her robe and pushes it off her shoulders. I lick my lips as I stare at her heavy breasts and her hard pink nipples. Rules be damned, she needs me. I reach up and take one nipple between my fingers, and roll.

Her head rolls back, and she moans. "Giovanni, please."

"What do you need?"

She slips off my lap and kneels before me on the bench. She cups her breast and brings it to my lips. I take her nipple and suckle.

"Yess," she draws out as she rubs her thighs together. I will allow it today because she has been so good at following my rules. Her mewls and moans fill the room. Her orgasm is building, demanding to be released.

My mouth reluctantly disconnects from her hardened nipple, leaving a trail of saliva as I push her back onto the bench. With ease, I lift her leg, revealing her glistening and slick pussy. My primal instincts take over as I spread her lower lips, exposing her swollen clit. I can feel its heat and pulsing desire under my touch. The delicate folds of flesh are adorned with wispy blonde hair, a tantalizing invitation that lingers in my mind but is quickly discarded. In this moment, there can be nothing between me and her delicate skin, every sensation heightened to an intense degree.

"Giovanni, I need, I need," she whines, lifting her hips upward.

I lift my fingers to my parted lips, still dripping with the sweet liquid. My tongue eagerly darts out to taste the remnants, savoring the indulgence that fills my senses. It's as if a burst of heaven has exploded on my taste buds, leaving me craving more. Oh my God, nothing has ever tasted this divine and satisfying.

"Do you need to come?"

"Yes, so badly."

Frustration and desire war within me as I take several deep breaths, knowing I am about to break yet another rule. But at this moment, with no one around to judge or witness, I give in to my primal urges. My hands shake slightly as they land on either side of her thighs, gently pushing them apart. As I lean down, the scent of Angelina's arousal hits me like a wave—the sweet and tangy driving me wild with need. My nose trails up her slick lips, reveling in the taste and feel of her. A moan escapes her lips, and she lifts her hips, silently begging for more.

"Does that feel good?" I whisper, and she moans in response. Removing my hands, I lift my head so I can see her. She is staring at me and moving her hips. "Tell me, I only want to hear you."

"Yes, it feels good. So good."

Her eyes widen in surprise, and she lets out a sharp gasp as I flick her sensitive clit with my skilled tongue. "What about this?" I teasingly trace a finger up the length of her velvety folds before gently pushing inside, mindful not to go too deep. "Does this feel good?"

"It feels so good," she pants, "please don't stop."

A wide grin spreads across my face as I continue to tease and lick her pulsating clit. With each stroke, I feel her body shudder with pleasure. As I push my finger in and out of her slick pussy, I can feel her walls tightening around me. My thumb joins in on the action, gently rubbing against her back wall, causing her to let out soft moans. My erection is throbbing, demanding attention, begging to be inside her. The anticipation is almost unbearable as I imagine the sensation of being buried deep within her. Just the thought of pounding into her until she screams my name sends a surge of desire through my body. Time seems to stand still as we both crave the moment when our bodies will finally be united in passionate ecstasy.

"Oh God, yes," she breathes. Her hips arch up, and I know she is close to her peak. I bite down on her swollen clit hard.

"Oh, God, yes," she screams. Her juices fill my mouth, and she shakes.

I put my hands on her thighs and hold her until the trembling subsides. "Giovanni. Giovanni," she murmurs like she is saying a prayer.

I reach down and pull her naked body to me. "I am here," I whisper into her hair. I rock her back and forth until her breathing returns to normal.

"Thank you," she says.

"You are very welcome. Now let's find you something to wear to lunch. I need you to look pretty for Daddy."

"I want to look pretty for you," she says with a smile.

I pick up her robe and hold it out for her to put on. We walk over to the closet, and I look at the dresses. I take the blush lace sheath dress with a sheer top and long sleeves. It was a classic dress that would look stunning on her. I hand her the Manolo Blahnik nude pumps with a crystal buckle.

I opened a few drawers before finding what I was looking for, matching the dress with a blush bra, panties, and a garter set with nude stockings.

"Come, let me help you dress," I say, holding out my hand.

She takes my hand, and I gently help her get the bra on. I hold her panties against her skin. She steps into them, and then I pull them up her legs. I roll her stockings up her legs until they are on her hips. I hook the garter belt on her hips, then move her panties over so the garter hooks can snap onto the stockings. I lean down and kiss her hips before slowly bringing my mouth to her pussy. I give her slit a gentle kiss. "You smell so good."

"I want to feel your mouth again," she says.

"Liked that did you?" I ask with a smirk.

"Yes, very much so," she answers as her face heats up in her signature blush.

God, I hope she never loses that. I hold out the dress, and she steps in. Before I zip her up, I place a kiss on her back. When she has her shoes on, I walk with her in her bathroom, and she applies her makeup while I brush her long, silky hair. I want it down today so I can reach out and touch whenever possible.

When she is dressed, I pull out the box in my pocket. It was a set from the Genovese family jewels. It was one of the few sets that didn't have red diamonds or rubies. This set was a stunning diamond choker, diamond stud earrings, and a diamond tennis bracelet. I stood back and took her in. She looked like the queen that she was. Damn, I was so lucky.

She looks at herself in the mirror, and her hands go to the necklace. "It is too much, Giovanni."

"You will be a Genovese in a few days, and nothing is too much. Now come, your father is waiting, and I have invited a friend to join us," I say.

"Who?"

"Davide Bonanno. He is a good friend of mine."

She is quiet for a moment. "Is he another mafia leader?"

"Yes. He is one of the five founding families," I say.

"Doesn't the public think you are enemies?" she asks.

"Yeah, and no. Davide and I have always been close. We go out a lot with each other. I think you will like him."

I offer my arm, and she wraps hers around it. We head downstairs to find Charles and Hamm waiting. I look at Hamm and tilt my head. His movement is so slight no one would catch it unless they were looking so intently. He shakes his head, and I know they didn't find out who sent the email.

"Angelina, you look lovely," Charles says, kissing her cheek.

"Thank you, Daddy. Look at the beautiful necklace, earrings, and bracelet Giovanni gave me.

"They are beautiful," he says and looks at me. I can see the worry in his eyes. If something happened to Angelina, he and I would not survive.

I know Hamm has already called the IT team to begin working on who sent the email and making The Famiglia aware of the threat. We have a threat level system, and this wouldn't be a level one threat level, but it did move to level four.

The ride to lunch was filled with Charles sharing funny stories of Angelina when she was growing up. Her blush just intensifies with each tale. She was so into the stories she didn't notice the black SUV in front and behind us.

We pull up in front of the Tavern of the Green. Hamm and the other security detail ensure everything is safe before opening the door. Charles steps out, and I follow him. Even though I know the area has been checked, I also check. When I felt she was safe, I reached inside the car for Angelina. She places her delicate hand on mine and steps out.

A few pardons passed us, and I caught a few men staring at her. I growl menacingly as I pull her closer. She is mine and mine, Drago says deep inside.

"Wow, will you look at that stunning woman with that loser," someone calls out.

I turn, ready to pull my gun and shoot the fucker when I see Davide. "You asshole," I growl, hitting him in the arm.

"What? She can do much better than you," he says with a smirk and steps closer to Angelina. He reaches down and takes her hand, bringing it up to her lips. "Davide Corvo Bonanno."

"Oh, Davide, it is a pleasure to meet a friend of Giovanni," she says politely.

"Oh, the pleasure is all mine. Now if you tire of this asshole, remember I am available," he says, wiggling his eyebrows.

Angelina giggles and blushes.

"Fuck man, does she do that all the time?" Davide asks.

"Yes," I answer.

He leans close and whispers. "How the fuck do you resist it?"

"It is hard, very fucking hard," I answer. He knows I am talking about my dick.

He laughs out loud. "Let's go have some lunch." Then, he walks over to Charles and shakes his hand. He walks in with him as Angelina and I follow behind.

"I like him," she says.

"More than me?" I ask.

"Never, Giovanni," she answers, her eyes full of truth.

So that is why he selected the red dress. Oh my, I was going to stand out like a sore thumb. I wasn't used to being around strangers, and tonight, I would be in the spotlight.

"Are you going to announce the engagement?" Daddy asks.

"Yes. I have already informed the council of the engagement. All those in attendance who haven't heard through the press will be told tonight."

"What did your father say?" Davide asked.

"I haven't yet," Giovanni says.

Giovanni hadn't spoken of his family. "Does your father live close by?" I ask.

"No. He retired and is living in Rome, enjoying the good life. My aunt and cousins live nearby. They will be in attendance tonight and look forward to meeting you. They know of the engagement."

Doubts crept into my mind as I sat beside Giovanni, surrounded by his friends. What if they saw through my facade and didn't like what they found? Would I ever truly fit in with them? But I plaster on a smile, hoping to blend in and ignore the gnawing doubts in my mind. Yet, I couldn't help but lean into Giovanni for reassurance in this unfamiliar territory.

"I look forward to meeting them," I said softly, even though it was something that scared the living life out of me.

As the dessert was placed in front of me, my stomach twisted into knots. The anticipation of the upcoming ball weighed heavily on my mind. With all the preparations and expectations, I wasn't sure if I was truly ready for such a grand event. Part of me longed for it to be over already, while another was filled with excitement and nerves.

Giovanni must have noticed my nerves because he squeezed my hand reassuringly. "Don't worry, Angelina. I'll be by your side the entire night."

I nod, feeling grateful for his presence.

Giovanni pays the bill and escorts me out of the restaurant. When we step outside, I cringe. The damn paparazzi are here again. How do they keep finding out where we are?

"Fuck!" Davide says. "Giovanni, we have a bigger issue than the paps."

Giovanni stands tall and protective in front of me, like a shield against the young men approaching us. They are dressed in expensive suits tailored to perfection and hold cigars between their fingers with arrogant confidence. Their polished appearance gives off the impression of GQ models, but their predatory gazes reveal their true intentions. It's clear they have no honorable plans for us.

"Well, well, well. Look what we have here," one sneers, eyeing me up and down.

Giovanni takes a step forward, his eyes flashing with anger. "What do you want, Dom?"

"Just a little chat with the Raven," Dom says, blowing smoke in Davide's face.

I feel Giovanni tense up beside me, his hand tightening around mine.

"I don't have time for this," Davide says, attempting to walk past them.

But they block our path, their smirks growing wider. "You think you can just ignore us, Raven?"

Davide takes a step closer to the man in the middle. "Dom, you don't want to start something."

"I just have a proposition for you," Dom says, a wicked glint in his eye.

"I'm not interested," Davide replies, his voice cold and hard.

"You haven't even heard what we have to offer," another man says, stepping forward.

"He said he is not interested," Giovanni snaps, his grip on my hand never faltering.

The men exchange a look before one of them speaks. "Fine. But don't say we didn't warn you."

With that, they step aside and let us pass. I let out a breath I didn't realize I was holding as we made our way to the car.

"What was that all about?" I asked, my heart racing.

"Just some old acquaintances," Giovanni says, his voice tight.

"Are they dangerous?" Daddy asks, concern etched on his face.

"They're nothing we can't handle," Giovanni replies, but I can tell he's not entirely convinced of his words.

As we got into the car, I tried to shake off the fear I felt. I glance over at Giovanni, wondering what he's thinking. He's always been so guarded, never letting anyone see his true emotions. But at that moment, as he stares out the window with a furrowed brow, I can see the worry etched on his face.

"Giovanni, who were those men?" I ask softly, placing a hand on his arm.

He looks at me then, his eyes softening. "Just a few guys from Russia."

"But why did they act like that?" I press.

He sighs, running a hand through his hair. "It's complicated, Angelina. Just know they're not good people, and I don't want you anywhere near them."

I nod, feeling a bit uneasy. I wasn't sure what was going on, but I trusted Giovanni.

We arrived back at my home, and Giovanni walked my father and me to the door.

"Charles, the moving boxes have arrived. Please have your staff start packing Angelina's artwork and supplies.

Shit, I had forgotten about the packing. "Angelina, pack what you want to take immediately to Genovese estate. Once we are married we can move the rest. Then I want you to take a long bath before the hairdresser comes and helps you get ready for tonight. I'll be here at seven to pick you up. You know what to do if you have any questions or concerns."

"Call or text you," I answer without hesitation.

He gives me one of his sexy smiles and my core clenches. With a glance at my father, he leans close and skims his hand up my dress to my panties.

"What am I going to do with you, ruining all your panties?" he whispers.

His finger slides back and forth. I reach out and grab his arms for support. "Stop it," I breathe, trying to keep my composure in front of my father.

Giovanni pulls away, his eyes dark with desire. "I can't help it, Angelina. You drive me crazy. I'll leave you now and will see you at seven."

I lean up on my toes and place a quick kiss on his lips. "I'll be the woman in red."

He fists his hands, and I can see him fighting himself to leave, making my heart beat faster.

Yesterday was a hard day for me. His punishment hurt like hell, but now, I get why he did it. I only wished he could have stayed with me last night. And as much as I hated the idea of another spanking, I knew it would happen, but then we would be married, and he would stay with me afterward.

He gives me a wink, turns on his heels, and walks to the car. I stand on the steps and watch until he disappears down the driveway. I take a deep breath and head upstairs to do as I am told. After removing my dress, heels, and stockings, I put on a pair of joggers and a matching top. It is too nice to pack, but Giovanni would be mad if he knew I wasn't wearing his clothes.

Ten boxes later, I have packed everything in my room except what I would need to wear tonight. However, I was still determining what I was doing tomorrow and what I would need for the wedding on Saturday.

I take out my phone and text Giovanni asking what I

should keep out for the next few days. Seconds later, a list of what I needed not to pack came back. The list was confusing, and I wondered what I would be doing. I just had to trust Giovanni was going to take care of me.

I gently turn the faucet knob, releasing a stream of hot, steamy water into the porcelain tub. I add a generous amount of bubble gel, watching as it instantly transforms the clear water into a frothy sea of suds. Stripping out of my clothes and stepping in, my body is warmed as I sink into the depths. My head gently rests on the plush pillow at the end of the tub, and I feel the tension from the day begin to melt away under the soothing heat. The scent of lavender and peppermint fills the air, transporting me to a state of pure relaxation. This is my sanctuary, my escape from the chaos of the outside world.

Submerged in the warm, sudsy bubbles of the bath, my mind wanders to Giovanni and the intense rush of emotions he ignites within me. The way his touch effortlessly commands and explores my body sends shivers down my spine, both exhilarating and terrifying in its intensity. With each breath, I am consumed by his presence, unable to resist the alluring pull towards him. As I soak in the tub, a sense of longing washes over me, yearning for his strong embrace and dominant control over my heart and soul.

A deep sigh escapes my lips as I close my eyes, letting my thoughts drift to the man who would soon become my husband. My heart flutters with nervous anticipation, wondering if I am truly ready for the role of his wife. Would I be strong enough to endure the trials and tribulations of this life?

"Mr. Genovese, we have a problem?" Hamm says, coming into my office carrying a large envelope.

"What is it?" I ask, dreading what it might be.

"This was dropped off at the gate while we were at lunch," he explains.

I open the envelope and pull out a stack of pictures. As I look at the first one, my blood runs cold. It is of Angelina and me on the bench in front of the window before going to lunch. She is naked in all of them, and her face is clear to see. However, you can't make me out as the man with his face between her legs. Or the man who was lapping her nipples as she offered her breast to him.

"Who saw these?" I growl.

"Just me, sir, and only the first one briefly, I swear," Hamm stutters. I look at his eyes and know he is telling me the truth.

"Did they detain the person who dropped them off?" I ask, my blood boiling.

"No, sir. The person came on a motorcycle, threw the envelope at the gate, and drove off. We got a plate number on the bike. We are running the number as we speak," Hamm says.

If these photos got back to The Commission, Angelina's reputation would be destroyed, and they would deny me marrying her. The founding sons of The Famiglia had rules the other members didn't have to abide by. It ensured the sons weren't taken advantage of by women who used their bodies to get them to marry them. There was no divorce in The Famiglia for the founding sons.

"We need to find out who sent these and make sure they don't get to the commission," I say, racking my hand through my hair. I need to be proactive to ensure I have the backing of other commission members in case the pictures make it to them.

I take out my phone and send a text to fellow founding sons.

> Giovanni: Need a meeting outside the council ASAP.

> Davide: When and where?

> Luca: Count me in.

> Andrea: Do I need to kill someone?

> Danti: Make sure you have enough bourbon.

Reading the message allowed me to take a breath I didn't know I was holding. We are not blood relatives, but we are still family.

> Giovanni: The warehouse in one hour.

I could have brought them here, but if someone is surveilling the Greco estate, they are probably mine as well.

But who is doing this? Is it the cartel? The email to Charles appears to be his old enemy, The Corporation. But why now? Just because Angelina has been seen outside the walls shouldn't have stirred up the cartel vendetta.

"Is Maeto still in prison?" I ask.

"Yes. He is in maximum security and is only allowed outside of his cell one hour a day. They deny him any visitors or any communication going in or out," Hamm explained.

I don't trust the prison system. It is too easy to pay off guard to smuggle information in and out. Hell, we do it all the time. But something about this doesn't seem like something The Corporation would do. Fuck, they would have already tried to take Angelina out.

"Hamm, I want you to put men on Consigliere Morgan. Also, start digging into his life. I want to know everything, even down when he takes a piss."

"On it, boss," Hamm says, taking out his phone and typing a message.

"Have the Range Rover out front in fifteen," I say.

Hamm raises his eyebrow. "Sir, you are not thinking about going out alone, are you?"

"Yes. We are going to do a little shell game. I want you to take the Bentayga and drive around. I'll take the Rover and go in the opposite direction," I explain.

Hamm hesitates for a moment but then nods his head. "Understood, sir. I'll make sure to stay in contact with you."

I grab my coat and head towards the door, the pictures burning a hole in my pocket. As I drive away from the estate, I can feel the tension in my body rising. I need to find whoever is behind this and ensure they never cross me again.

The warehouse is old, abandoned, and perfect for a secret meeting. As I pull up, I see the other founding sons waiting for me. I park the Range Rover and get out, my hand resting on my gun.

"Giovanni, what's going on?" Luca asks, his eyes scanning the area for any threats.

I take a deep breath. "I have a problem," I say simply.

"What is wrong?" Davide asks.

"An envelope of pictures was dropped off at the gate today."

"Who was in the pictures?" Luca asks.

Guilt eats at me because I know it is all my fault. If I could have kept my fingers or mouth off Angelina, this wouldn't be happening. I run my hand through my hair. "Angelina."

Every one of them tilted their heads and raised an eyebrow.

"Okay. She is naked," I say.

"Someone is spying on her when she is alone in her room?" Andrea asks, his brow furrowed.

"Spying, yes, alone, no," I say.

"Giovanni, what are you not telling us," Davide asks.

"FUCK! Alright, she is naked, and I am licking her pussy."

It only takes a moment before all of them break out laughing.

"Dude, that is fucking hot!" Luca says, shaking his head.

"Fuck you all. You would be just as angry and put out as I am," I say.

"She is a beautiful woman, and you are man enough to take her. I would be upset if those pictures got out, but shit, I would be the first one passing it around to my brothers," Andrea says.

I raise my hand and make a motion to slap Andrea, but he grabs my arm. I drop my arm.

"So, you broke the rule," Andrea says. "Why call the meeting?"

"If these pictures come before The Commission, they may refuse me the right to marry Angelina. Her reputation will be ruined, and she can never marry within The Famiglia."

They shake their heads and agree to my assessment of the situation.

"Yeah, and Consigliere Morgan was saying some weird

shit yesterday. If he saw those photos, he would vote against the marriage," Dante says.

"The fucker will not see those pictures if I can help it. However, if they make it to The Commission, I need your vote in my favor," I say, looking at each one.

"Sure, brother, but what happens if the other four consigliere vote against? That leaves it a tie," Luca says.

Damn, the reason why we have nine members on The Commission is because it prevents ties. Over the years, there have been some close votes, but never have there been a tie.

"I don't think The Commission can deny Giovanni his vote. You have the right to vote as much as we do," Dante says, smiling at me.

"Let me see the photos," Luca asks.

My head whips around, and a snarl leaves my lips. Fucking asshole is not seeing the naked pictures of my angel. My Angelina.

Luca raises his hands. "I give up. I don't care that she is naked. I don't care that you are licking her pussy. If anything, she is giving you a gift."

I take out the envelope, and a wave of relief comes. I was afraid that someone may have gotten to them.

Andrea laughs. "Take a picture and send it to all of us."

"Fuck you, fuckers." Andrea is always the joker in the group

I pull out the photos and place them on the old wooden table. The one on the top was the one where Angelina is reaching for her ankles while I suck on her clit. Her mouth is open, and a soft moan escapes. The photo is taken from a height so that her whole body is in the frame, but it is the mouth-watering pussy that has my mouth watering.

Luca looks at his eyebrows knitting together. "You can't make you out."

"Yeah, I know."

"Her father is an expert in AI, correct?" Luca asks.

"Yes. His new program is the next level in AI. What does this have anything to do with these photos, and who took them?"

"Because if these make it to The Commission, we can say they are not her. We can say someone is using AI to prevent you from marrying her," Luca says.

I nod my head. "That is a good idea."

"You need to tell her father," Luca says.

"WHAT?" I yell. Had Luca lost his mind. There is no way in hell I was going to tell Charles about his. He was new to The Famiglia, but he knew I had to keep my hands off Angelina until the wedding.

"He will need to say the photos are AI-generated," Lucas says.

"No way in hell," I say.

"You don't have a choice. If you don't, he will find out eventually, and he will hate you for not telling him," Luca says. "It is better to tell him from the start and get him on your side."

"What if The Commission won't believe him? It is his daughter." I ask.

"Hmm, he has a point," David says.

"Alright, the AI defensive is the saved as a last resort," Luca says.

I nod my head.

"Hey. I was reading over the rules and regulations," Danti says, holding his phone. "Nowhere does it say that a founding son can be preventive his vote on any matter."

"So if we need to vote, we will have the majority," Davide says.

I look around at the four of them. They didn't once make me feel they weren't in my corner.

"Thanks, brothers," I say.

They all nod. Words didn't need to be said because we all knew we would take a bullet for each other.

I am dressed in my finest tuxedo, walking up to the door of the Greco estate. I couldn't wait to see Angelina in her dress. Tonight, everyone in attendance will know I am getting married, and I won't have to say a word. The moment Angelina walks into the ball wearing a red gown, it will be like shouting to the rafters. I AM MARRYING GIOVANNI DRAGO GENOVESE.

Tonight's ball, Fire and Brimstone, was my family's event. Men can only wear black tuxedos, black shirts, and black ties. Women can only wear black gowns. The only time a woman is allowed to wear a different color, and our family's tradition, red, was when she was engaged to the family leader or married to the leader.

I straightened my red tie and adjusted my weapon before ringing the doorbell. Charles opens the door. He is dressed in his black tuxedo, wearing a cocky smile. The man was going to have the single women of The Famiglia swooning tonight.

"Looking nice there, Charles," I say with a wink.

He pulls at his tie. "It has been a long time since I have been in one of these."

"Is she ready?" I ask, anxious to see her. It has only been a few hours, but I feel like a junkie looking for their next fix.

As Charles opens his mouth, I hear the click on her heels. I look up, and coming down the stairs is my queen in red. She is stunning. The red dress's corseted sweetheart's neck hugged her amble breast. Her body was hugged by a sparkling sequin gown, with the slit high enough to show off her toned thigh. Fuck me, I am one lucky bastard.

When she gets to the last step, I admire her from the top of her head down to the red-painted toenails peeking out her high-heeled shoes. Her hair was pulled away from her face, leaving the back silky straight to her waist. The makeup wasn't overdone but did emphasize her eyes with dark eyeliner and mascara with her lips painted in deep crimson red.

I take her hand and bring it up to my mouth, placing a kiss. "You look amazing."

Her face blooms. "Thank you."

I reach into my pocket and take out the box. Tonight, she will be wearing the necklace and earrings my mother wore on the night of her engagement. The necklace was shaped like a dragon, with its scales covered in diamonds. The spine is made of emeralds, and its eyes are red rubies. In the claws of the dragon was a flawless heart-shaped diamond. I remember her wearing the necklace to the fire and brimstone ball every time. Mother passed away ten years ago, and I still miss her smiling face. She would have loved Angelina.

I take out the necklace and fasten it around her delicate neck. "This has been passed down from one Genovese queen to the next for generations. I know my mother is smiling down upon us as you wear it tonight."

"Giovanni," she says as she touches the necklace with reverence. "I am proud to wear it."

I place a sweet kiss on her lips and offer her my arm. Tonight was going to be exciting.

Giovanni Drago Genovese, and Miss Angelina Greco," he announces.

They pull the black curtains back, and the spotlight shines on us. I can't see the audience's faces, but as we walk forward, and as soon as people see Angelina's dress color, they gasp. All eyes follow us as we walk to the head table on a platform that overlooks the crowd. Only the leaders of the five families and their dates were allowed to sit at the table.

Davide, Luca, Andrea, and Danti stand as we step upon the platform. None of them have a date, which is not uncommon. Hell, this was the first time I attended an event with a date. Shit, she wasn't a date. She was my fiancée.

"Angelina, you look ravishing," Davide says with a smirk.

"Thank you," she replies.

I place my arm around her waist and pull her close. "Let me introduce you to other assholes of the five families." I point at each as I introduce them. "This Luca Leone Gambino, Andrea Lupo Colombo, and lastly Danti Orso Lucchese."

She looks at each one and smiles. "Let me see if my Italian is good enough to decipher the names. Luca, you are The Lion. Andrea, you are The Wolfe. And last, and I am sure not least, Danti, you are The Bear."

I couldn't help but smile. "Beauty and brains all wrap up in this one."

"Mr. Genovese, sir, it is time for your announcement," the master of ceremonies says.

"Let's do this so the ass-kissing can begin," I say with a smirk.

Luca and Danti stand on my right, while Davide and Andrea stand on Angelina's left. I am hoping Angelina gets to know Davide better. Tomorrow, when she goes for her virgin test, at least she will have someone she knows in the room.

The master of ceremonies slams his staff against the floor, the sound reverberating through the room like a clap of thun-

der. Silence quickly takes over, leaving only a cloud of anticipation in its wake. This was my cue.

The crowd grows still as I step forward, and the silence
thrums with anticipation. My voice echoes across the ballroom. "Fellow members of The Famiglia," I announce, my
gaze sweeping over the guests with a humbling authority, "I
am proud to announce my engagement to Miss Angelina
Greco. We will be married Saturday evening in accordance
with our established traditions and customs." I pause for a
moment, and when my gaze falls on Consigliere Morgan's
face, I see it twist into a mask of contempt. His disapproval
hangs in the air like oppressive smoke.

Angelina steps forward, giving off a regal persona. Her
back is straight, and she holds her head high, but she's shaking
slightly. I can feel it in the pressure of her hand on my palm.
She looks up at me with pride and love, and I'm struck by how
beautiful she is.

The room erupts into cheers and applause.

"Congratulations, Giovanni. You've made a fine choice,"
Luca says, clapping me on the back.

"Indeed, she is a beauty," Andrea adds, giving Angelina a
flirtatious smile.

I narrow my eyes at him. "Watch your mouth, Andrea."

Danti chuckles. "Ah, young love. How sweet."

I ignored his comment and turned to Angelina. "Are you
okay?"

She nods, smiling. "Yes, I'm fine. I'm just happy to be here
with you."

I kiss her hand. "I'm happy you're here, too."

Member after member comes forward to give me congratulations. I thank each one and wish this would hurry up and
finish. Several times, I look out among the crowd and see
Charles. He seems to be having a great time. As I thought,
several eligible single women were making their intentions
known.

The elected members of The Commission come up. Consiglieres Jackson Patterson, Sidney Williams, and Lee Butler greet me and Angelina with respect, befitting my station. They walk away except for Consigliere Peter Morgan.

"Giovanni," Consigliere Morgan says, his eyes fixed on Angelina. He seemed to be undressing her with his eyes.

"It is Don Genovese, Peter," I snarl. I twitched to pull my gun and end his life here and now.

"Now, now. Tonight is celebrating. I must say you are even more beautiful than your photos," Peter says, licking his lips.

Without a second thought, I push Angelina behind my back and pull my gun, placing it against Peter's forehead. "One more word, and we will need to elect a new consigliere," I growl through gritted teeth.

Peter's eyes narrow before he takes a step back, holding up his hands. "I'm sorry if I offended you, Don Genovese." He steps off the platform and scurrys toward the edge of the room.

I feel a shaking hand on my back, which causes me to lower my gun. I didn't take my eyes off Peter until he was out of the ballroom. With a deep breath, I turn and pull Angelina into my arms. Her body shakes as she softly sobs. I rub my hands up and down her back, trying to soothe her. Rage pulsates through me as I think of the pain Angelina is feeling. Tonight was supposed to be a special night, introducing to members of The Famgilia my future wife. However, Peter ruined it with whatever his agenda was.

Davide places his hand on my shoulder. "The team is already on him," he whispers close to my ear.

I give him a nod before placing a kiss on the top of Angelina's head. "Come, let's go get you cleaned up, and if you still feel like staying, we can do some dancing."

She pulls back, giving me a chance to look at her face. Her makeup was ruined by her tears, but she was still the most beautiful woman in the room.

"I would like to stay," she whispers.

"Good, so do I. There are some people I would like you to meet," I say. Luca steps over and does his best not to look like the scariest motherfucker you would ever meet. Of the five of us, he was the biggest. He was six foot four and weighed two-fifty or two-seventy-five, all muscle. If his size wasn't intimidating enough, the jagged scar across his cheek was. His presence in a room caused people to leave.

However, underneath his shield of intimidation, Luca was one of the most loyal and protective men I had ever met. He is like a brother to me, and I knew he would do anything to protect Angelina.

"Gio, Lucy is here tonight, and she is excited to meet Angelina. Maybe she can accompany her to the bathroom to assist her with fixing her makeup," Luca asks.

I look down at Angelina and give her a smile. "How does that sound? Lucy is your age, and I think you two have a lot in common. She is a photographer."

Angelina's eyes widened and sparkled. The reflected aquamarine hues within seemed to glow even brighter. They held a depth and vibrance that captivated all who had the pleasure of looking into them. "I would like to meet her," she says.

Luca leans down, trying to make himself look smaller, while his mouth turns up in a small smile. "I'll go get her."

Angelina nods but quickly looks away. Over time, I feel sure she will become comfortable around Luca.

As she stands beside me, her heart-shaped face is etched with determination. I can't help but be in awe of her bravery as she calmly faces the difficult situation at hand. It's moments like these that make me realize just how perfectly she complements me and my own strengths.

Moments later, Luca walks back towards us with his sister, Lucy, on his arm. She is tall slender, and could be a model. However, she must rather be on the other side of the camera. Luca was proud of his sister and did everything possible to ensure she was safe. She had a security detail that followed her everywhere. At first, she tried to buck at the intrusion, but when she was almost kidnapped by the Russians, she accepted this was going to be best.

"Lucy, I would like to introduce you to Angelina," I say, placing my arm around Angelina's waist and pulling her closer.

"Hello. I absolutely love the dress," Lucy beams.

"Thank you. Would you like to help me repair my face?" she asks.

"I would love to," Lucy answers. "Because we know these guys know nothing about makeup. Well, other than Davide."

I couldn't help but chuckle at the comment. Lucy was always poking jabs at Davide. She likes him, and if he would ever get his head out of his ass, he would admit he likes her too. When they finally admitted their feelings, it was going to take me, Danti and Andrea to hold Luca back. Because he is going to go nuts when he figures out that one of his best friends is in love with his little sister. Fuck, if I had a sister, I would probably be the same way.

Angelina and Lucy make their way to the bathroom, leaving me with the rest of the guys. I can feel their eyes on me, waiting for me to say something.

"That was a close call," Danti finally breaks the silence. "Peter is lucky you didn't pull that trigger."

"He won't be getting another chance," I say through gritted teeth. Peter had always been a problem, but I had kept him around because of his connections. But now, he had crossed a line that couldn't be uncrossed.

Luca clears his throat. "You know what needs to be done."

I nod. "I'll take care of it."

The rest of the night goes smoothly, the incident with Peter forgotten for the time being. Angelina and Lucy return to the ballroom, Angelina's makeup fixed and looking even more gorgeous than before. We dance the night away, and I can feel the eyes of the other members on me, on us.

But I don't care. In this moment, all that matters is the woman in my arms. Angelina's laughter is like music to my ears, and I swear I could dance with her like this forever. We spin and twirl around the ballroom, lost in each other.

As the night draws to a close, I escort Angelina back to my car. I can tell she's exhausted, but her smile never fades. However, the next two days were going to be hard for her, and I hope I can do everything I can to make them bearable.

Chapter Nineteen

ANGELINA

I can't believe I am getting married tomorrow. Last night was a roller coaster of emotions. First, I was excited about attending my first ball and the announcement of Giovanni's and my engagement. Then, the incident with the weird Consigliere Morgan. I know Giovanni is the head of the Genovese crime family, but seeing him pull his gun and point it at Morgan scared me. Then he put himself in front of me. He was willing to put his life in danger for me. It was then that I realized how much I loved him. He was my protector, my hero. But now, as I sit here staring into the mirror, I feel a sense of unease. Am I ready for this? Am I prepared to be married to a man who lives a dangerous life? A man who could be taken away from me at any moment?

A knock sounds on my door, and I hear my father call out. "Angelina, are you awake?"

"Come in, Daddy."

He walks in carrying a steaming cup of coffee. "I thought you might be needing this."

I sit up and take the cup from him. Hmm, it is just how I like it. "How are you this morning?" I ask.

"A little tired. I've not been to an event like that in a long, long time. Did you have fun?" he asks.

I couldn't help but smile. "Yes."

He brings over the chair from my desk and sits beside the bed. "You and Giovanni looked so good together on the dance floor. People were wondering about you and how you were able to catch on the founding sons. They didn't know who I was, and I found it very enlightening to get their unfiltered comments."

"I still can't believe this is happening."

"Are you happy?" he asks.

"I know it sounds impossible, but I love him. I still have much to learn about him and how this relationship works. However, I am sure I want it to work. The only thing that worries me is you will be alone."

He pats my leg. "Angelina, I have only wanted for you to be happy, and if Giovanni makes you happy, then so am I."

Someone knocks on the door, and when we look up, it is Hazel. "Mr. Greco, Davide, and Nan Bonanno are here to see you and Angelina."

Dad looks at me with his eyebrows knitted together. "Do you know why Davide is here?" he asks.

"No, and who is Nan? I thought Davide was single," I say.

"Well, I'll go downstairs and keep them company while you get ready," Daddy says.

"Okay," I say. When Dad leaves, I pick up my phone and notice a text from Giovanni. I looked at the time he sent it, which was at three a.m.

Good morning. I want you to wear the floral white dress with the white lace bra and panty set. Wear the white flats with the floral bow on top. Davide will be coming by and explaining what is happening. If I could prevent this, I would. As powerful as I am, this is a rule I can't break. Afterward, I have arranged for you, Lucy, and my cousin to have an afternoon at the spa. While you are away, the movers will be in to move all your stuff here. I will come over and have a quiet dinner with your dad tonight. Remember, you only have to call me if you have questions or concerns. Giovanni

Oh my. What was happening today that he wouldn't be there for it? Well, whatever it is, I will face it with the grace and dignity Giovanni's bride-to-be should have. After a quick shower, I dress as Giovanni instructed and head downstairs. Hearing voices from the living room, I find Davide and an older woman sitting on the couch, drinking coffee.

"There she is," Davide says, standing and walking over. Placing a kiss on my cheek and grasping my hand. "Come over and let me introduce you to my mother."

Nan was Davide's mother. As I near, I can see the similarities. Her Italian heritage's rich, golden hues radiated from her olive-toned skin, set off by piercing, crystal-blue eyes. Her shoulder-length locks were flawlessly styled and fell in waves of dark brown that shimmered almost black in the light. But upon closer inspection, one could see subtle strands of silver grey interwoven throughout, giving her hair a unique and striking appearance.

She stands and brings me into a tight hug. "It is such a pleasure to meet you."

When she lets go, I smile at her. "The pleasure is all mine."

"Davide told me you were a beauty," she says, looking toward Davide with a look of love and pride. "Now, meeting you, I am sorry he didn't meet you first."

Davide chuckles and grasps her hand. "Mom is always trying to marry me off. She wants grandbabies while she is still young so she can spoil them rotten."

I have to still myself as I see the interaction between them. The love of my mother was something I never had. Daddy always showered me with love and support, but seeing them together showed me what I had missed.

"Angelina, Giovanni asked us to come here today to explain the rules of The Famiglia concerning what has to happen when a member or a founding son gets married," Nan says. "Daughters born into The Famiglia are taught the rules when they are old enough to understand. Since your father just became a member, you didn't have the opportunity to learn."

"Is there a difference between a founding son and a member getting married?" I ask.

"Yes," Davide answers. "When the five founding families formed The Famiglia, they put in place a group of strict rules for themselves so they would be held to a higher standard."

"So some of these rules are about marrying?" I ask.

Nan gives me a small smile. "Angelina, a woman who marries a founding son, is also held by these rules and standards."

"Giovanni had to come before The Commission and asked for their vote of approval on the engagement," Davide says.

"What is The Commission?"

"It is the ruling board of The Famiglia. They are judge, jury, and executioner," Davide replies.

My heart races as Davide explains more about The Commission. It sounds like something out of a movie, but this is real life. I am about to marry into a world where The Commission holds all the power. "So, what does this mean for me?" I ask, trying to keep my voice steady.

"It means that you will be under their watchful eye,

Angelina. They will ensure you uphold the values and traditions of The Famiglia. You must always show respect and loyalty to The Commission and your husband. You must be careful of what you say and do because your actions reflect on Giovanni, the entire Genovese family, and The Famiglia."

My mind is spinning with all the information. This is not the fairy tale wedding I had imagined. But as crazy as it might seem, I have fallen head over heels in love with Giovanni and am willing to do whatever it takes to make this work. "What do I have to do?" I ask.

"Today, you have to prove you are untouched and pure for Giovanni," Nan answers.

The comment hits me like a punch to the gut, causing a knot of fear and confusion to form in my stomach. My voice shakes as I ask, "What the hell does that mean?" I can feel my heart racing, adrenaline pumping as I wait for their response, bracing myself for the worst.

"It means that you will have to undergo a virginity test to prove you are pure for Giovanni," Davide explains, looking at me sympathetically.

My heart sinks as I hear the words. A virginity test? Is this some kind of sick joke? "I don't understand why I have to do this," I say, my voice shaking with anger and disbelief. "Why should my worth be determined by whether or not I'm a virgin?"

Nan comes over and puts a hand on my shoulder. "It's not about your worth, Angelina. It's about upholding the values of The Famiglia. They cannot have a founding son or a member marry a woman who is not pure. It would bring shame and dishonor to his family and The Famiglia."

I feel tears prick at the corner of my eyes. I didn't know that getting involved with Giovanni would mean submitting to this kind of test. But I also know that I cannot lose Giovanni. He is everything to me. "Alright," I say, my voice barely above a whisper. "I'll do it."

Davide's gaze, heavy with empathy and understanding, pierces through me. Nan gently holds my hand and guides me through the unfamiliar steps of the test, her voice soothing and reassuring. She tells me that a compassionate female doctor will oversee the procedure to ensure my comfort and ease any anxieties I may have.

"Normally, a male doctor from The Famiglia performs the test, but Giovanni refused to allow any male to touch you. He called in one of the few female doctors of The Famiglia to perform the test," Davide explained.

Alright, I could do this. It was just like having my yearly exam. Daddy always had female doctors come to the house to treat me. "When is she coming here?"

"Angelina, the test has to be done at The Famiglia compound," Davide says.

"WHAT?" I yell. "Please tell me it will be just the doctor in the room."

I stare into Davide's eyes, and I see pain in them. "There has to be a witness in the room," he says.

A desperate plea escapes my lips as I turn to face Nan, my eyes pleading for her to confirm my deepest desire. "Please," I beg, holding onto a sliver of hope that it might be her. My heart races as I wait for her answer, praying that she will be the one who stands by my side.

She shakes her head. "It has to be one of The Commission members," Davide says.

"Who is on The Commission?" I ask.

"Myself, Giovanni, Luca, Danti, Andrea and the four consigliere. However, Giovanni can't be in the room or even on the compound."

Racing thoughts and emotions flood my mind as I try to think who would be in the room. Would it be Morgan standing there, ready to scrutinize me and ensure my purity? The anticipation and fear clashed inside of me.

"Angelina, Giovanni asked me to be the witness," Davide

tender skin above your heart. He will be the one responsible for etching ink into your flesh, leaving an indelible mark upon your body."

My heart races in terror as I realize what is about to happen to me. How can someone still do this in the modern world? It's like being trapped in the dark ages. My voice shakes with fear as I plead, "Is he even capable of doing a tattoo?" Sweat beads on my forehead as I wait for an answer, dreading what might come next.

"All of the founding sons are taught how to do it and do it with minimal pain," Davide says.

"So after the tattoo, is that it?" I ask.

Nan shakes her head. "Your restraints will be removed, and you will kneel before Giovanni. This is where you pledge yourself to him. You must say Padrone del mio cuore, corpo e anima, Master of my heart, body, and soul. After which, you kiss his family's ring."

Okay, that was a little degrading, but not as bad as it could be. Daddy had already told me about me I would have to say the pledge to my husband. Yesterday, I let it slip when I was still emotional after coming down from the spanking he gave me. But something tells me the worst hasn't been revealed.

"Charles, I think it might be best if you stepped out," Davide says.

Daddy's eyes dart between him and me, his face twisting in a mixture of pain and anger. The weight of his emotions seemed to physically crush him, each breath more labored than the last. I can feel my heart racing as I try to decipher the source of his torment.

"Go, Daddy. Nan and Davide will explain this part," I plead.

He shakes his head but stands and walks slowly out of the room.

"This is bad, isn't it?" I ask.

With tears streaming down her face, Nan nods in affirmation. She takes a moment to compose herself before continuing, "Have you ever delved into the intricate customs and expectations placed upon royalty during the dark ages when it came time for them to consummate their marriage?"

"No."

"In The Famiglia, the founding sons are royalty and must show proof of the consummation."

I was terrified to ask, but I knew it would happen whether I knew about it or not. "How?"

"The sides of the marriage bed are draped in white silk fabric. The bride and groom get into bed, and once they are naked, The Commission members surround the bed. When the husband penetrates his wife, breaking her hymen, he withdraws and presents his blood-covered shaft to the members," Nan explains.

Nausea rises in my throat as I imagine what it will be like. My mind reels with the inhumanity of it all, screaming out against the cruelty that no one should ever have to endure. And then it hits me like a physical blow: "Did you suffer through this too, Nan? Was your innocence also ripped away?"

Nan unbuttons the top of her blouse with a delicate hand and pulls it back, revealing a large tattoo of a fierce raven. The inked lines are dark and bold against her pale skin, showcasing her strength and courage. "Yes, Angelina," she says, her voice full of empathy. "As painful as it may be, this is the last time Giovanni will allow anyone to see you in such a vulnerable state."

"Angelina, Giovanni hates the thought of anyone seeing you. However, this is how it has been since the beginning," Davide explains.

A wave of nausea hits me like a freight train, and I stumble to my feet, gasping for air. My body convulses with violent spasms as I frantically race to the bathroom. Collapsing to my knees, I heave and gag until there is nothing left in my stomach but bile and agony. Every muscle in my body screams in torment as I crumple to the floor, drenched in sweat and tears.

I daydreamed about my wedding day since I was a little girl. It would be a sunny, picturesque day filled with love and joy. My father would proudly escort me down the aisle, his eyes brimming with emotion as he gave me away to my beloved groom. As we exchanged vows and rings, the sun would shine down on us like a blessing. Afterward, we would celebrate with a lavish reception filled with music, laughter, and delicious food. Our first dance as husband and wife would be a magical moment, surrounded by our loved ones. We would share bites of cake and sips of champagne, each one sweeter than the last. In that moment, all of my dreams would come true as I am finally united with my soulmate in marriage.

However, Giovanni's dragon flew down, setting fire to all my dreams. There would not be one moment of my wedding I would want to remember.

Tears pour out my eyes as I grieve for the loss of my dreams. A few minutes later, I heard footsteps approach the door. "Angelina? Are you alright?" Nan asks, and when I don't answer right away, she opens the door and enters.

"Nan, you don't want to see this," I say.

"Sweetheart, I have seen worse over the years," she says, rubbing her hand up and down my back.

Her statement of seeing worse made me shiver. Davide, like Giovanni, was the head of their family in the mafia. Were the rumors about the violence they were part of true?

But now was not the time for questions about their past. I needed to focus on the present, on what was happening to me, and find a way to escape this horrible fate that awaited me. My mind raced, searching for a glimmer of hope, a plan to defy the traditions that bound me.

"Nan," I whispered, my voice trembling. "Is there any way out of this? Any way to avoid this consummation ritual?"

Nan sighed heavily, her face filled with sorrow and regret. "Angelina, I wish there was. But this is deeply ingrained in our traditions, our way of life. It's not something we can easily escape."

My heart sank, my last shred of hope fading away. The reality of my situation crashed down on me like a ton of bricks. How could I have been so blind? How could I have allowed myself to be trapped in this web of darkness and control?

"Sweetheart, are you okay?" my father says outside the door. No wonder Davide wanted him out of the room when they told me about the consummation ritual.

"Nan, can you go talk to him? I will try to pull myself together."

"Certainly, dear," she answers, patting my back.

As she quietly leaves, I find myself collapsing, unable to hold back tears. The constant battle in my head rages on. Why can't Giovanni just be an ordinary man? Why does he have to be involved in something that degrades and humiliates women? My love for him constantly clashes with my morals, leaving me torn and conflicted.

Despite the overwhelming suffering, one thing remained constant—my all-consuming love for Giovanni. I had never known another man aside from my father, yet the touch of his hand ignited a fire within me that could not be extinguished. My heart beat only for him, and in that fleeting moment, I knew he was the only one who could ever possess it.

Getting on my feet, I wash my mouth and hands in the sink. The cool water calms me somewhat, but I still feel nauseous. More tears stream down my cheeks when I turn around to look at my reflection. The undeniable truth of my impending doom floods my heart with sorrow. I open the door to find Davide standing outside, waiting for me.

settles in my stomach, like a heavy stone weighing me down. Something about this moment doesn't feel right.

"Angelina, I know this is awful, and I promise you, like I promised Giovanni, to make it as painless as possible."

Reluctantly, I give her a slight nod and shuffle my feet towards the table. My heart races as I see the step stool next to it. Climbing onto the tall table makes me feel vulnerable and exposed. Part of me wants to retreat, but another part knows I have no choice if I want to complete this task. So, with a deep breath, I reluctantly use the stool and hoist myself up onto the table.

I settle onto the table. The coolness of the metal sent a shiver down my spine. I could feel my heart pounding in my chest, the sound echoing in my ears. Dr. Bianchi approaches me. Her gaze is gentle yet unyielding.

"Angelina, I need you to lie back and place your feet into the stirrups," she instructed softly.

I bit my lip, my hands trembling as I complied with her request. The vulnerability of this position sent a surge of fear through me, but I knew there was no turning back now. Davide's absence gnawed at me, leaving a void that only intensified my anxiety.

As soon as I was settled, Dr. Bianchi moved to the end of the table, adjusting the stirrups to hold my legs in place. Her touch was gentle and professional, but it did little to ease the tension that coiled within me.

"Alright, Angelina. I am going to get Davide, and we will get this horrible business over with."

I close my eyes and force myself to calm down. Giovanni's choice of Davide was calculated. They were more than just friends. They were bound by a fierce brotherhood that extended beyond blood. A bond forged through shared sacrifices and unbreakable loyalty. A bond that would drive them to protect each other and their families at any cost, even if it meant laying down their lives.

"WHAT THE FUCK DO YOU MEAN?" screams Davide.

"I am going to be the witness," a man says. The voice sounded familiar, but I couldn't place it.

"Dr. Bianchi, what is going on?" I ask.

"I don't know," she answers.

"YOU CAN'T!" Davide yells. "LET GO OF ME."

Panic courses through me as I desperately try to sit up, my feet pinned down by the cold, unyielding metal stirrups. The sound of the door bursting open echoes in the small room, and suddenly, Consigliere Morgan storms in with two towering figures draped in ominous black suits. My heart thuds against my chest, betraying my fear as I realize I am completely at their mercy.

"What is the meaning of this?" Dr. Bianchi exclaims.

Consigliere Morgan's voice slices through the room like a razor, his accusation sharp and deadly. His predatory gaze fixates on me, sending shivers down my spine. "It has come to The Commission's attention that Miss. Greco's claim of being pure is nothing but a lie," he declares, each word dripping with disdain as his eyes bore into mine. My skin crawls under his intense scrutiny, and I feel exposed and vulnerable in front of this powerful man's judgment.

"I don't know what you are talking about. My virginity is intact," I declare in a voice stronger than I have ever heard myself use before. "Where is Davide? He is the one Giovanni selected to be the witness to the test."

"With the evidence we have, Mr. Genovese's choice had to be removed. I am going to be the witness of the test," Consigliere Morgan says with a wicked grin.

"Consigliere Morgan, sir, this is very unusual," Dr. Bianchi says.

Consigliere Morgan walks toward Dr. Bianchi and grasps her arm hard. The pain she feels is shown clearly on her face. "I could have you thrown into the prison cells under The

Commission chambers and leave you there to rot. Now perform the test," he commands and nods to the two men. They walk over and hold my arms down on the table. I am now completely at his will.

My body recoils in terror and disgust as Dr. Bianchi's hands invade my most private space. But the horror of her touch is eclipsed by the overwhelming dread that floods me when I glimpse Consigliere Morgan looming behind her. His gaze fixated not on my face but on my exposed and vulnerable body. My heart pounds in my chest as I realize that this intimate violation should only be witnessed by one man, my Giovanni.

"Angelina, I am going to insert the speculum. It is cold and hard. You will feel some pressure and discomfort," Dr. Bianchi says, her face showing concern for me. This wasn't her fault, and when I get out of here, I will make sure Giovanni knows this.

I grit my teeth and squeeze my eyes shut, attempting to block out Consigliere Morgan's insidious presence. But the weight of his intense gaze still lingers on me, taunting and challenging me. What cruel motives lie behind his actions?

I feel the cold metal, and my inner walls clench over the intrusion. Moments later, I feel it removed and I sigh with relief. It is over.

"Consigliere Morgan, she is a virgin," Dr. Bianchi says as she stands and moves to block his view from my most private part.

"I don't believe you," he snarls, reaching out and pushing her. Her head rams into the edge of the table, slicing open a large gash to her forehead. She collapses to the floor. Consigliere Morgan rushes forward and sticks his fingers in me.

I scream out from both pain and embracement. "STOP, STOP, STOP," I scream.

With a forceful jerk, he yanks his finger out, and I am

relieved to think it's over. But then he plunges them back inside me with such viciousness that it feels like my insides are being ripped apart. His jagged fingernails rake against the delicate walls of my pelvis, tearing and shredding as if intent on destroying me from within. Each thrust sends waves of excruciating pain through my body, leaving me feeling like a helpless victim in the face of his relentless attack.

The predatory glint in his eyes sends shivers down my spine as he lunges towards me, intent on taking what is mine. My heart races, and I struggle against the two hulking men holding me down, their grip like iron vices around my wrists. But with my feet trapped in the cold metal stirrups, there is no escape from this violation, and my mind goes blank with fear and despair. This will affect not only my engagement with Giovanni but also my innocence and sense of self-worth.

My heart pounds against my ribcage, on the verge of exploding from the overwhelming anticipation. The air is thick with tension as I await my fate. Suddenly, the door explodes open, and Giovanni and Davide storm into the room like a hurricane, guns drawn and fury etched on their faces. Their unrelenting gazes lock onto mine, blazing with the fire of righteous rage as they witness the atrocities that have been inflicted upon me. Without hesitation, Giovanni pulls the trigger twice, unleashing a barrage of bullets that shatter through the air like a deadly symphony. The goons fall to the ground. My body floods with primal adrenaline as I realize I am no longer alone in this brutal fight for survival.

"Giovanni, you are not allowed to be here. You have voided the test," Consigliere Morgan declares with his fingers still inside of me.

Giovanni's eyes spark with malice as he raises his gun, aiming it directly at Consigliere Morgan's forehead. "Step back, or I'll blow your brains out," he growls, his finger itching to pull the trigger and end Morgan's life in a split second.

Consigliere Morgan's fingers retract with a sickening

squelch, and as he holds them up, I see the crimson liquid coating his fingers. My vision blurs with tears as I realize what has happened; my innocence, my purity, has been ripped away in one brutal act. The pain in my heart is overshadowed by the crushing weight of my future crumbling before me. No longer a prized possession to be given away in marriage, I am now nothing but damaged goods, unwanted and disposable in the eyes of The Famiglia.

"Well, it looks like we don't have to worry about the test after all," Consigliere Morgan says with an evil chuckle.

The tears cloud my vision but I see Davide rushing over and capturing Consigliere Morgan. He tries to fight against Davide's hold but he is no match to Davide's size and strength.

Then I feel a hand against my cheek. I flinch away.

"Shh, my love, I am here," Giovanni murmurs.

"I'm sorry. So sorry," I cry.

"There is no reason to be sorry. This is not your fault," he says softly, like a warm blanket.

"But I am no longer a virgin."

"We don't know that for sure. Let me get you off this table," he says.

"How can I not be? I saw the blood."

"Angelina," Dr. Bianchi says.

I look over and see her getting off the floor. Her forehead was still bleeding. She picks up a cloth and dabs at the cut.

"He may have only torn the soft lining inside your inter walls," she says.

"How will I know for sure?" I ask.

"The only way is for me to do the exam again," she says.

"No. She is not going through anything else," Giovanni growls. "She has been through enough."

"She is ruined, and I will tell all the other members. You can't marry a woman who is not a virgin," Morgan says. "But I will take the damaged goods off your hands."

"Get him out of here," Giovanni growls.

"No," I say. "Dr. Bianchi, do the test."

"Angelina, baby, you don't have to do this," Giovanni says.

"Can you marry someone who is not a virgin?" I ask. He wants to say yes, but I see the turmoil in his features. The rules of The Famiglia are impended in his every cell.

"Dr. Bianchi, let's get this over with," I say.

Giovanni's grip on my hand tightens as he brings it up to his mouth, his breath warm and heavy against my skin. With a feather-light touch, he kisses my knuckles, his eyes never leaving mine. The intensity of his gaze sends shivers down my spine as if I'm being consumed by a fire that only he can control.

When I feel Dr. Bianchi begin the exam, I look at her.

"No, keep your eyes on me," he commands.

I turn my eyes back to his and pray for a miracle.

Chapter Twenty-Two

GIOVANNI

I sit beside Angelina as Dr. Bianchi checks to see if she is still a virgin. She shouldn't have to go through this again. However, as much as I wanted to say, it didn't matter. Under the laws of The Famiglia, it did. Being a leader, I had to abide by the rules, and Angelina knew that. It was a burden we both carried, but one that had been ingrained in me since birth. The Famiglia demanded loyalty and adherence to their archaic customs. But as I watch Dr. Bianchi examine Angelina, a surge of anger courses through me.

Angelina clenches her fists tightly, her face pale with fear. I could see the pain and humiliation etched into every line on her delicate features. She deserves better than this; she deserves freedom from the chains that bound her to our world.

Dr. Bianchi finished her examination, her eyes flickering with relief as she relayed the results. "She is still intact. His fingernails must have torn the soft lining, but it already has begun to heal."

But even though it confirmed her innocence, it did little to soothe my burning rage. When I received the call from Davide, I felt my inner dragon come to life.

I couldn't be on the compound during the test, but I didn't

want to be too far away. Ever since the call from Davide when he advised me how Angelina took the news of all the things she would have to endure to marry me. When he said she had become physically ill, I wanted to rush over and pull her into my arms. I knew if I did, I wouldn't be able to release her to go to the exam. So, instead, I went to the compound and sat across from the gates.

The exam shouldn't take too long, and as soon as she was done, I would meet her outside the spa. I needed to feel her in my arms to ensure she was okay.

As I wait, I think about where I want to take her for our honeymoon. We could go anywhere in the world. It was my decision to choose where. However, I wonder where she would like to go.

Suddenly, my phone rang. I looked at the screen to see it was Davide and immediately knew something was wrong. I answered the call with a sinking feeling in my chest. "Davide, what's happened?" I demanded, my voice strained with worry.

"You have got to get here now," he exclaims.

"HAMM, TAKE ME ONTO THE COMPOUND," I yell. "Davide, what is happening?"

"Morgan has kicked me out of the exam. Two of his personal goons are in the room with Angelina," Davide explains.

"What do you mean, kicked you out of the room?" I ask as Hamm speeds through the gate and up the drive.

"He burst in and told me he was going to be the witness. Then, two guards grabbed me and pulled me outside. They are standing guard at the entrance."

"FUCK!!" I yell. I look up and see we are close. Seconds later, I see Davide standing where he said he was.

I jump out of the car and rush over to him. "We are going in there." Hamm opens the trunk, and we each pick up another gun.

We rush towards the entrance. I see the two goons, and

without a second thought, I place a bullet between their eyes before they can even raise their weapon. No one was going to stand in my way to get to Angelina. The door to the security crashes open, and two of the regular guards rush out. They look down and see the two bodies on the ground.

"Mr. Genovese, you are not allowed on the property today."

My eyes narrow as I glare at the guard, my rage simmering just beneath the surface. "I don't give a damn about your rules," I growl, my voice dripping with lethal intent. "Move aside or suffer the consequences."

The guard's face pales, realizing the gravity of the situation. He exchanges a nervous glance with his companion before reluctantly stepping aside. I don't waste any time storming past them.

Davide follows closely behind. "Gio, we need to think this through," he urges, attempting to reason with me.

But I am beyond reasoning. My only thought is to reach Angelina and ensure her safety. I ignore Davide's pleas, my footsteps echoing through the hallways as I navigate through the labyrinthine corridors of The Commission compound.

With a ferocious determination, I reached the door to the room where Angelina was being subjected to the virginity test. My hand grasps the doorknob, only to find it locked. But no mere lock could stop me from reaching her. Stepping back, I channel all my rage and strength into one powerful thrust as I slam my shoulder into the ancient wood. The door splinters and gives way, and with Davide at my side, we burst into the room. My heart seizes at the sight before me. Two men were holding Angelina down while Morgan was defiling her with his fingers.

An inferno builds inside me, raging and roaring like a feral dragon. My inner beast, Drago, demands to be unleashed from his prison within my soul. I have kept him chained, refusing to let him consume my emotions. But now, with a primal scream, he breaks free. Without hesitation, I aim and fire a single shot straight between the eyes of the creatures holding Angelina captive. They crumble to the ground with a resounding thud. And then, with a menacing growl, my dragon's attention turns to Consigliere Morgan, ready to unleash hell upon anyone who dares stand in our way.

When he raises his fingers, and I see her precious blood on them, my heart stops. He had ripped her future away from her. Never in my life had my hand shaken when I pointed my weapon. Davide rushes forward and captures Morgan, pulling him away from Angelina. He drags him to the corner of the room, where Hamm places zip ties to his hands.

I glance down and notice tiny droplets of crimson staining the crisp white fabric. What would have happened if I hadn't gotten here in time?

"Giovanni," Angelina says, her voice so whisper soft it felt like an angel wing on my skin.

She looked so tiny on the table. Her face smeared with tears. I think she is so frail and helpless. Then she asked for the examination to happen again. The strength and determination I saw in her eyes matched some of the most ruthless men in the world. When Dr. Bianchi tells us she is still a virgin, I feel the weight of my responsibilities dissipate.

I turn to her. My dragon purrs at her beauty. He knows she has not been taken for us. She will be ours forever. "Yes, my beauty.

"I'm scared," she says, glancing over to where Morgan was standing.

I turn to Davide. "Take him to the cells and lock him away."

"YOU CAN'T DO THAT!" Morgan yells. "I'M A CONSIGLERE."

I stand and walk over. "By the laws of my founding family, you can and will be held. You have touched a founding son's fiancée, had a founding son's witness removed from a test

without the founding son's permission, and damaged a
founding son's property. You will be brought forth to The
Commission for trial for those offensives."

"I am The Commission," Morgan says.

"No, you were on The Commission. By the rules, you can't
be on The Commission with a pending trial," I grin. "Hamm,
take him away and notify the other members of The
Commission."

I walk back over to Angelina. She looks so small and
breakable. If I were a better man, I would let her go. Let her
find someone who would love her and treat her like the angel
that she is. But I can't let her go.

I lean down and place a soft kiss on her lips. "Let me help
you up and get you dressed. I'll take you home."

"But I want to go to the spa if I may," she says.

I had figured after all this excitement, she wouldn't want to
be around people. "Are you sure?"

"Yes. I don't want someone asshole to ruin the rest of my
day. Tomorrow will be tough, and I've never had a spa day."

"Well then, my brave queen, let me get you to your spa," I
say with a smile. Looking around the room, I see Dr. Bianchi
and Davide standing by the door. "If you will excuse us."

"Certainly, Mr. Genovese," Dr. Bianchi says and walks out.

"I'll stand watch by the door," Davide says. I hadn't
thought of that. There was no door now after I torn through
it earlier.

"Where are your clothes?" I ask Angelina.

"Behind the screen, but I can get them."

"No, you stay there. I'll be right back with them." I walk
around the screen to find her dress, panties, and shoes. A smile
breaks out when I notice she is wearing exactly what I
instructed, except where was her bra? Carrying the items, I
come back to the table and lay them beside her. "Did you
forget to put something on today?"

Her forehead furrows. "No."

"Where is your bra?" I ask.

"I have it on. I figured I didn't need to remove to have a virginity test."

I break out in laughter. "Smart girl."

She blushes and looks away, her fingers fidgeting with the edge of the sheet. "I didn't know what to expect. I just wanted to be prepared."

I shake my head, still chuckling softly. "You never cease to amaze me, Angelina." I reach out and gently tuck a stray strand of hair behind her ear. "But let's get you dressed so we can get out of here."

With utmost care, I help her sit up and slip on the dress, my fingers grazing her bare skin, sending a shiver down both our spines. The sight of her in the delicate white fabric, coupled with the vulnerability in her eyes, ignites a fire within me that demands to protect and cherish.

As she slipped on her shoes, I noticed a tear in her soft-spoken demeanor. "Are you all right?" I ask, my voice laced with concern.

Her eyes meet mine with a mix of gratitude and vulnerability.

"I will be," Angelina whispers, her voice barely audible. "But... I don't know if I can ever forget what happened in this room."

My heart clenches at her words, and the fire within me burns even brighter. The need to shield her from any further pain and darkness intensifies. Without hesitation, I wrap my arms around her, pulling her into a protective embrace. She rests her head on my chest, seeking solace in my presence.

"Angelina," I murmur, my voice filled with determination. "I promise you, no one will ever hurt you again. I will do whatever it takes to keep you safe."

Her grip on me tightens like she's clinging to the hope I offer. We stay like that for a moment, finding strength in each other amidst the chaos surrounding us.

Eventually, we pull apart, my hands still finding comfort in holding hers. Her eyes meet mine once more, and a newfound resolve flickers within them. The events that just transpired have left their mark on her, but I can see that she is determined to rise above the darkness. At this moment, I realize the depth of her strength, and it only intensifies my desire to shield and protect her.

"Thank you, Giovanni," she whispers, her voice steady and filled with a newfound determination. "I know there will be challenges ahead, but I'm ready to face them with you by my side."

A surge of pride swells within me as I gaze into her eyes. She has endured so much, yet she remains resilient. It fuels my determination to ensure that no harm ever befalls her again.

"I won't let anything or anyone hurt you, Angelina," I vow, my voice filled with conviction. "We will face whatever comes our way together. And we will come out stronger on the other side."

The slight smile tugging at the corners of her lips infuses her face with a radiance that warms my soul. Her trust in me is a gift that I will always cherish, and I will do everything in my power to live up to the responsibility it entails.

"We make quite the team, don't we?" she murmurs, her voice filled with a newfound sense of hope.

I nod, unable to tear my gaze away from her beautiful face. "Yes, we do. Together, we are unstoppable."

With that, we leave the room, leaving behind the remnants of a painful past. As we make our way through the dimly lit corridors of the building, Davide falls into step beside us. Their unwavering and loyal presence offers a sense of security that envelops us like a protective shield.

Once we reach the exit, I guide Angelina towards the waiting car, opening the door for her like a true gentleman. She slips inside gracefully. I turn to find Dr. Bianchi behind us.

I reach out my hand toward her, and we shake. "I want to thank you for all you did for her in there."

"I'm sorry I couldn't stop him," she says.

"He was a man on a sick mission. You will have to testify at the hearing."

"Of course. If Angelina needs anything, please let me know. She is a remarkable young woman," Dr. Bianchi says.

"Thank you." She was right. Angelina surprises me at every turn, and I can't wait until she is mine completely.

Chapter Twenty-Three

GIOVANNI

"I promise I won't leave the building without my guards," Angelina says, kissing my lips quickly.

I pull her close, feeling the heat of her body against mine, and whisper in her ear, "Be a good girl," I growl, my voice low and commanding, "or I will spank your ass so fucking red that every movement will be a reminder of my dominance over you." Her breath hitches as she imagines the sharp sting of my hand on her skin, making her tremble with both fear and desire. A primal thrill runs through me at the thought of showing her who is in charge.

She gasps, and when I look into her eyes, I don't see fear. I see something that surprises me -excitement. Damn, she is so fucking perfect. I slap her ass and quickly leave her before I say the fuck with it and stay by her side. However, this has to be done. The entire commission, excluding Morgan, has been summoned to report to the compound to be advised of the situation. Dr. Bianchi has written a statement of events, and Davide would give first-hand details. I hope Angelina won't have to appear before The Commission until after our wedding.

The damning evidence against him was irrefutable. Yet

the final piece of the puzzle that sealed Peter Morgan's fate was the surveillance camera discreetly positioned in the exam room. It was installed this morning. Suspicion had been brewing since Morgan's unsettling comments last night, and I couldn't shake the feeling that he was up to something sinister.

My fiery dragon, Drago, roars within me, clawing at the bars of his cage with ferocious desperation. He longs to break free, fueled by the images of our beloved Angelina being harmed by the likes of Morgan. He wants to exact his revenge upon those who wronged her.

My car glides to a stop in front of the grand commission chambers. As I step out, Hamm rushes over and hands me my cloak. It is a symbol of my position in The Famiglia. My cloak is a rich shade of crimson red, lined with black satin. The large hood obscures my face, adding an aura of mystery to my presence. On the left side, right across my heart, is the intricate embroidery of The Famiglia coat of arms, a mark of our allegiance and loyalty. The other members of The Famiglia also wear cloaks during special events, but theirs are all black, contrasting my vibrant color.

Wrapping the cloak over my shoulders, I pull open the door and walk inside. When my great-great-grandfather and the other founding sons designed this building, they did so to strike fear into anyone who walked in.

The dimly lit chamber was adorned with intricate tapestries and ornate chandeliers, casting eerie shadows across the room. The air was heavy with a mixture of anticipation and tension as I made my way towards the front, my footsteps echoing off the marble floors.

I near the table I find I am the last one to arrive. As I glance at each member besides Davide, I see they need clarification about why they were called.

"Gentlemen, thank you for coming on short notice. We have a serious situation which involves Peter Morgan," I say.

"Giovanni, what has happened?" Luca asks. I see the concern written all over his face.

Each breath is a struggle, my chest heaving with the weight of my emotions. My heart pounds violently against my ribcage, fueled by a mixture of rage and fear that threatens to overpower me. With shaking hands, I force the words out in a frantic rush. "Peter Morgan violated Angelina during her virginity test this morning," I declare, each syllable laced with palpable disgust and searing anger. The accusation hangs heavy in the air, suffocating us with its gravity and truth.

The air is thick with shock and disbelief as every face in the room contorts into a mask of horror. In all my years, there has never been a consigliere who dared to commit such a heinous act against one of our founding sons. The very thought of it sends chills down my spine.

"Consigliere Morgan?" Consigliere Butler asked. "Are you sure?"

How dare he ask such a stupid question. Would I call a meeting without having just cause? I fist my hands and breathe in deep through my nose.

Davide's voice booms through the room as he stands, his eyes flashing with determination. "Gentlemen," he declares, "I was there, and I will give you my firsthand account of what happened." He slams a signed affidavit from Dr. Julie Bianchi onto the table, the sound echoing like a gavel in a courtroom. "And I have evidence to back up my words," he adds, his jaw set in steely resolve. All eyes turn to the document, hearts racing with anticipation for the truth to be revealed.

Each member began reading the documents. I watch their facial expressions to get a read on their feelings with the information.

"Giovanni, is Angelina okay?" Luca asks.

"She is doing okay considering the situation," I answer. "We ask the daughters of The Famiglia to undergo an exam to prove they are worthy of becoming our brides. The exam is degrading, and they feel helpless during it. Today, my future bride went into the exam with the grace of a queen. She didn't have the privilege of learning what we expected as a daughter of The Famiglia, like most young girls do. Her father only pledged himself and his family to The Famiglia. Yet she did as we asked and climbed on the exam table, thinking she would be safe. However, we let her down. There is another piece of evidence which will prove, without a doubt, of Peter Morgan's guilt."

Davide stands and pushes the remote to lower the screen. Seconds later, the video begins. I will myself to remain calm as I watch. I knew from the information Davide, Dr. Bianchi, and Angelina, but as the other members, this would be the first time I had seen the video.

As the video plays, every second feels like an eternity for Angelina. I grit my teeth. My fingers dig into the edge of the table as I watch in horror as Morgan violates her. Every fiber of my being screams for revenge, to make him suffer agonizingly for what he did to her. When the video gets to the part where I bust in and Morgan holds up his bloody fingers, everyone in the room gasps. Davide shuts off the video and gives me a sympathetic nod.

With a fierce glint in his eyes, Davide slammed his fist on the table. "Listen up, gentlemen," he bellows, his voice drips with venom. "Peter Morgan is guilty of unlawfully detaining one of our founding sons and causing irreparable damage to the property of Don Giovanni Genovese." His words hung in the air like a heavy cloud, daring anyone to challenge his authority.

"Don Genovese, do you have anything else to add?" Consigliere Lee Butler asks.

"No."

"Then we should set a time for the trial of Peter Morgan," Consigliere Lee Butler says. "I believe it should be done without delay."

I stand. "I want to wait until after the wedding."

"What wedding?" Consigliere Butler asks.

"My wedding," I answer.

"Angelina is no longer a virgin, so you can't marry her," he says.

I look toward Davide, who pulls out the exam results after the attack. "Gentlemen, Angelina went through a second exam after the attack, and this is a signed result from Dr. Bianchi. Angelina Greco is still a virgin."

"How?" Consigliere Butler asks.

"If you read the document, you will see that Morgan only tore the soft lining of her inner walls with his fingernail," I say, my jaw clenched.

A sudden hush fell upon the room as the members read the document, and the implications of the situation became clear. Consigliere Butler's face turned pale, and he quickly shook his head in disbelief.

"This is unacceptable," he said, his voice shaking. "We must take swift action and ensure justice is served."

"What is your word, Don Genovese?" Consigliere Butler asked, looking to me for guidance. "What do you want us to do?"

Memories of Angelina flood my mind, and I am consumed by guilt. I made a promise to protect her, but in her most vulnerable moment, she was hurt. Tomorrow is meant to be a day she looks back on with joy, but I know she will carry the scars from my inaction. I may not be able to change the tattoo or commitment ceremony, but I can do something to ease the trauma on her wedding night. It's the least I can do after failing her so miserably.

My voice booms through the dimly lit room as I declare, "I invoke the ancient rite Sangue per Sangue." My fellow founding brothers' eyes widen in awe and admiration, knowing the power that this rite carries. Only once before in The Famiglia's dark history has this rite been called upon.

While the founding sons knew the rite, the elected members seemed to be confused.

"I am sorry, Don Genovese, I have never heard of this rite?" Consigliere Patterson asks.

Fury boils in my veins as I watch them stumble through The Famiglia's sacred rituals and rites. These are the leaders meant to govern and guide the members, yet they are ignorant of our most fundamental laws. How can we trust their leadership when they don't even know the rules? It's a mockery, a disgrace that fills me with a searing rage. "Sengue per Sengue, means Blood for blood. I give up my right to inflict justice against Peter Morgan for the right to have my consummation private."

"You can't ask for that. It is required by the laws which govern the founding sons," Consigliere Butler states.

"You don't understand," I growl. "The ancient rite demands that I, as the injured party, may choose the method of justice. There will be no trial, no courtroom drama. I want to relinquish my vengeance, allowing the justice to be handled by whomever you vote to do so, and in doing so, I am granting Angelina the privacy and dignity she deserves."

There is a moment of stunned silence as the words sink in. Consigliere Butler looks at me, his face a mask of outrage and shock. But then he nods reluctantly. "You have invoked the rite, and we have no choice but to follow the ancient laws. Very well. We will make the necessary arrangements for your consummation to be recorded and notarized, proving your right to the blood owed to you. But know this, Don Genovese: you are playing a dangerous game. By choosing your justice, you risk everything. Are you sure you want to give up your right to justice for a woman?"

My fist crashes down on the table with a resounding thud, my entire body trembling from the fire of anger burning inside me. How dare he speak so coldly of Angelina, my beloved betrothed? My voice booms through the room as I

"You belong to me," he snarls before crashing his mouth onto mine with violent force. The kiss is not sweet or gentle. It is a possession, a show of dominance for all to witness at the wedding. The pressure of his lips against mine is suffocating, branding me as his forever in front of everyone.

He finally pulls away, and I have to grip his arm to prevent myself from collapsing. "Wow."

He leans down and whispers in my ear. "Oh, baby, you haven't seen anything yet. Now, let me put my mark on you."

He wraps my arm around his and walks us down the aisle. He walks out the chapel doors, and Hamm is waiting, who hands Giovanni a black cloak. Giovanni places it around my shoulders, pulling the hood over my head. Hamm hands him another cloak, this one a deep red, and he puts it on, pulling the hood up. We walk down a path to a walkway between the buildings. Ahead, I see it open up into a court-yard. This must be where the tattooing ceremony was going to be held.

Giovanni stops and opens a door to a room. He ushers me in and pulls back both our hoods. "We need to wait until The Commission has taken their places."

"Oh," I say.

"Nana and Davide explained this part, right?"

"Yeah," I say as I try my best not to let my nerves get the best of me. I clutch my hands in front of me, trying to control their shaking. Why was this so hard? I thought I would be terrified at the wedding. However, I was calm during the whole thing.

"Angelina," he says, wrapping his big hand around mine. The energy that always follows when we touch sends an instant feeling of relief. I look up into his deep, soulful eyes. "I can't promise you that it won't hurt, but it is not as bad as I am sure you are imagining. Some people find getting a tattoo actually enjoyable. The pain causes your body to release endorphins, which many find sexually stimulating."

Did he just say people got aroused by getting a tattoo? "Do you have a tattoo?" I ask.

"Many of them," he answers with a wicked grin.

He has many. Oh, my God, I can't wait to see them. I think to myself. Where and what were they? My body reacts to the thought of his tattoos. My core clenches and I feel my panties become wet. I feel myself flush with the thoughts.

Giovanni leans down and licks the shell of my ear. His hot breath sends shivers and goosebumps down my body.

"I promise I will take care of you and make sure you are as comfortable as possible," he assures me, his voice a deep, soothing rumble that ripples across my skin. "And when the ceremony is over, and we are home in our bedroom, you will see all my tattoos."

As he speaks, his hand grazes down my arm, and I can't help but shiver at his touch. He is right. His mere presence can make my body respond in ways I never imagined. My heart flutters like a trapped bird as I take in the intensity of his gaze.

The anticipation of the tattooing ceremony is both exhilarating and nerve-wracking. As I stand there, hand in hand with my new husband, I can't help but wonder about the bedding ceremony later this evening. My stomach flips at the thought of others watching Giovanni and me in bed as we have sex.

Suddenly, I hear a church bell ring three times, and the door to the room opens. Two men in dark cloaks with hoods pulled up so far that I can't see their faces. They are holding long wooden staffs with a metal emblem on top. Before I can make it out, Giovanni steps in front of me and pulls up my hood.

"Stay strong, Angelina," he whispers, his breath ghosting over my ear. "We are in this together."

I take a deep breath, trying to steady my nerves. This was it. Giovanni pulls up his hood, and we follow the two men out.

Giovanni's strong hand grips mine, and I feel the warmth and comfort in his touch.

As we enter the courtyard, I see the small wooden chairs arranged in a semi-circle around a wooden platform with a bench in the middle. The two men stop and flank either side of the steps which lead up to the platform. They place their staffs in front of them, and as the bell chimes once more, they lower their heads.

Giovanni takes my elbow and guides me up the steps. We stop when we are beside the bench. I see the cuffs dangling off the sides like Nana said they would be. Giovanni grasps my clock and pushes it off. The chill of the night air causes me to shiver. He motions for me to lie down on the bench, and I do so without delay. Once I am lying flat, he cuffs my hands and feet.

"Angelina," he says, his voice firm and commanding. "You are about to take one of the most significant steps in your life. This tattoo ceremony will mark you as my property and signify the start of our life together as a married couple. It is a bond that cannot be broken, and I promise to guide you through it all."

Nana instructed me that I was to remain silent until it was time for me to say my pledge. I glance over, and I see those who were in attendance in the same color cloaks as Giovanni. They were seated, and due to the hoods, their faces were not visible. I turn back and watch as Giovanni uncovers a table where the tattoo gun and ink are located.

Giovanni removes his cloak, reaches down, and unbuttons the lace from the top of my gown. He pulled it back so the skin above my heart was unencumbered. He picks up a piece of paper, and I am unsure what it is until he places it on the skin. It was then I realized it was the stencil for the tattoo. He adjusted it several times before he was happy with the placement. He rolls the table closer and flips a switch. The buzz of the machine starts as he picks up the tattoo gun, adding what must be ink to it.

He brings the tattoo needle down and I jerk at the pain.

In a voice so low only I could hear, he says. "Stay still."

My teeth sink deep into my lip, drawing blood as I try to suppress the moans escaping my lips. With each prick of the needle, a wave of sensation floods my body, igniting a fiery pleasure that consumes me. Time becomes irrelevant as Giovanni's skilled hand moves across my skin, etching his masterpiece onto my body. I never want this feeling to end, to be lost in the blissful agony for eternity.

The searing pain slowly dissipates as Giovanni applies a cool, soothing substance to the raw, inflamed skin. Antibacterial cream, I realize. He carefully wraps a bandage over the area, his touch gentle yet firm, and the agony is forgotten for a moment.

He rises to his feet and violently shoves the table aside, looming over me with a ferocious glare. My wrists and ankles are freed from the cuffs, but I am still reeling from the effects of the needle coursing through my body. As he helps me sit on the bench, I look up at him, trembling under the intensity of his gaze. His breaths come in ragged gasps, his nostrils flaring with every inhale. With a sudden jolt, I notice the massive bulge straining against his pants. Holy fuck, he's enormous.

With calculated grace, he strides towards the platform's edge, where a regal crimson throne awaits. With a flourish, he throws back his cloak and sits. He beckons me to him, a command that I can't resist. This is the moment I've been waiting for, the chance to pledge my unwavering loyalty to him. Padrone del mio core, corpo e anima, Master of my heart, body, and soul. His words echo in my mind as I gaze upon him sitting on his throne, every fiber of my being acknowledging him as my one true Master. I feel an overwhelming need to display my complete submission to him, so I drop to my knees and crawl toward him with reverent determination. My head remains bowed in humble obedience as I await his next command.

Time slows to a crawl as I wait, my heart pounding in my chest and my breaths coming out in shallow gasps. Suddenly, his hand reaches out and strokes along my jaw, pulling my face towards him with a fierce grip. My body trembles as I gaze into his face, feeling both fear and desire coursing through me. He places his ring finger close to my lips, and without hesitation, I press a kiss onto his family's crest. The metal is cold against my lips but ignites a fire within me, an unbreakable bond between us. As I lean back on my heels, looking up at him with reverence, I speak the words that bind us together: "Padrone del mio cuore, corpo e anima," Master of my heart, body, and soul. My voice is strong and resolute, declaring my unwavering loyalty to him.

Chapter Twenty-Five

GIOVANNI

Each word she spoke was a dagger, plunging deep into my chest and twisting until my heart was in shreds. The conviction in her voice, I know for sure, made the other members of The Commission turn green with envy, seething with jealousy at the thought of me being the one to marry this goddess at my feet. I am overwhelmed with gratitude that it is I who holds her hand, knowing I may never be worthy of such a fierce and untouchable love.

I stand and offer her my hand, which she takes without delay. Once she stands, I wrap her cloak around her delicate shoulders, and we walk down the steps past the sentry who protected us during the ceremony. We pass by The Commission and head toward the car. It was time for us to go home. I couldn't wait to get her out of the gown and naked in our bed. Our bed. The bed where I will take her virginity. The bed where I claim every part of her.

As we enter the luxurious car, I can feel the weight of expectation settling upon my shoulders. The air inside grows heavy with anticipation, mingling with the scent of her intoxicating perfume. Sitting beside her, I steal glances at her delicate profile, her eyes fixed on the passing cityscape outside.

She is a vision of elegance and grace, a woman destined to ignite the flames of passion within me.

The car glides through the streets, each turn bringing us closer to our shared destiny. In these moments, amidst the silence enveloping us, doubts begin to claw at my conscience. Am I truly deserving of her affection? Can I be the man she needs, capable of fulfilling her deepest desires? The weight of my responsibilities as a member of The Commission threatens to crush me, reminding me of the choices that brought us together.

Her fingers brush against mine, sending a shiver down my spine. In that simple touch, I find solace and reassurance. She believes in me and trusts me with her heart and her body. I cannot let doubt consume me. I will rise to the occasion for her.

The car pulls up to our grand estate, its imposing gates opening to welcome us home. As we step out, the servants line the entrance, their eyes filled with admiration and respect. Now, they see the woman by my side. Tomorrow, I will introduce her to everyone, but now I need her naked and in our bed.

I lead her through the grand entrance, our footsteps echoing against the marble floors as we approach the opulent staircase. The crystal chandeliers overhead cast a warm glow upon us, illuminating her radiant beauty. I can see the servants stealing glances at us, their eyes filled with awe and reverence. They have witnessed the transformation that has taken place within me, as if I have been reborn into a man worthy of her love.

We ascend the staircase hand in hand, the anticipation building with each step. The door to our bedroom looms before us, inviting and intimate. As I push it open, a wave of familiarity washes over me, reminding me of the countless nights spent dreaming of this very moment.

The room is adorned with rich tapestries and soft candlelight, casting shadows that dance along the walls. The scent of roses fills the air, mingling with her intoxicating perfume. A four-poster bed beckons from the center of the room, its luxurious white sheets inviting us to surrender to our desires. I turn to her, and our eyes meet, a silent understanding passing between us. This is the moment we have been waiting for.

Her hand trembles in mine as we cross the threshold into our private sanctuary. The air is heavy with anticipation, charged with a raw, magnetic energy that binds us together. I close the door behind us, shutting out the world and sealing our fate within these walls.

Without a word, I step closer to her. My gaze fills with a mixture of reverence and adoration. I gently brush the back of my fingers against her soft cheek, feeling the warmth radiating from her skin. Her breath hitches ever so slightly as she leans into my touch, a silent affirmation that she has chosen me as her partner in this dance of passion.

Her brows furrow as she takes in the room. She was told what to expect the room to look like for the consummation. However, none of it is here.

"Giovanni, where is everything?" she asks. "I thought we had to prove I was pure, and we consummated our marriage. Nan said it was a rule of The Famiglia."

"It is. However, I invoked an ancient rite, which allowed us to spend our first time together alone."

"I am confused," she says.

I guided her delicately over to a quaint wooden table that had been adorned with a simple but elegant spread. Margaret thoughtfully laid out a light dinner for us amidst the chaos and excitement of the day. In all the commotion and rushing around, I hadn't even realized my hunger until now, and I couldn't help but wonder if Angelina felt the same. "With all that's been going on, I'm sure we're both in need of sustenance," I remark as we settle into our seats. I gesture towards the array of dishes before us. "Let's eat while I fill you in on everything."

Carefully, we fill our plates with the delectable dishes. The succulent aromas waft through the air, and my mouth begins to water in anticipation. I pour each of us a generous glass of crisp white wine, the liquid glowing in the soft candlelight. Raising our glasses in unison, I could see Angelina's hand trembling slightly as she, too, toast to the moment. "To us," I say, the words carrying weight and meaning as we clink our glasses together and sip the refreshing wine.

She smiles, and I see how it lightens up her entire face. We are almost finished enjoying our food and wine when I decide she needs to know. I need to tell her why we can celebrate without a room full of people.

"Yesterday, after your attack, I called The Commission together."

"Oh. Why did you need to do that?" she asks.

"It is a rule that if someone is held in the cells, The Commission members have to be made aware immediately. But it was even more serious since a consigliere was being held."

She takes a big drink of her wine. "Did they believe you?"

"Davide and I presented all the evidence. Once they heard everything, they declared Peter Morgan to be held until trial. Unfortunately, you will have to testify during the trial," I answer.

With tears streaming down her face, she curls up into a ball and starts to tremble. Helplessly, I rush to her side and lift her, carrying her to the bed and holding her in my lap. As she clings to me, I struggle with my conflicting emotions. I want to comfort her, but I also feel overwhelmed by her distress. I am in control of all things in our relationship and household. Never in my life have I felt anything like I do for her, but I don't know what it is.

Her voice trembles with fear as she pleads, "Do I have to

see him?" Her hands grip my jacket so tightly that her knuckles turn white, the fabric crumpling under her desperate hold. She's like a drowning person clutching at a life preserver, desperately trying to keep herself afloat in a sea of anxiety and dread.

"Yes, however, he won't be able to touch you, I promise," I say. The fucker will never touch her again. I pull her closer, wanting her to feel safe.

"Giovanni, what rite did you invoke?"

"Sangue per Sangue," I answer.

Her brow furrows deeply, her eyes narrowing in concentration as she struggles to decipher the words. "Blood for blood?" she repeats, her voice trembling with fear.

"Yes. By the rules of The Famiglia and The Commission, the founding son who was wronged has the right to carry out the punishment. However, I am giving up my right for blood, so when I take your virginity, it can be in private," I explain.

Her eyes grow wide, and her mouth falls open. "You did this for me?"

I give her a wolfish smile. I stand, and I place her on her feet. Taking her hand, I take her into the bathroom and start the shower. "Turn around," I say. She does it without hesitation, which pleases me. I unzip the gown and push it off.

Her bare back is exposed to me, delicate and vulnerable. I reach out, running my fingers along the curve of her spine, tracing invisible patterns against her skin. A shiver courses through her body, a mixture of anticipation and desire. Dropping the gown to the floor, she stands before me in nothing but her tiny lace thong, a vision of breathtaking beauty.

I step closer, pressing my body against hers, feeling the heat radiating between us. My lips find the nape of her neck, placing gentle kisses along the sensitive skin. She exhales a soft sigh, surrendering to the intoxicating pleasure that courses through her veins.

I reach around and cup her full breasts in my hands,

feeling their weight and softness against my palms. Her breath quickens as I caress them with tender strokes, teasing her nipples and causing her to moan softly. She tilts her head back, offering me her lips in a silent plea for more, her body begging for my touch.

I turn her around, brush the hair from her face, and gaze into her blue eyes, swimming with desire and love. Our connection is electric, a bond that transcends words and time.

I rip off my clothes, never breaking my intense gaze with hers. My body is on display for her, every inch of skin on fire and pulsing with desire. She takes her time to absorb it all, her eyes roaming slowly over all my tattoos as she commits each detail to memory. But when she reaches my straining cock, her reaction is electric. Her pupils dilate, her breaths quicken, and goosebumps ripple across her skin. The raw intensity between us crackles like electricity, sending shivers down my spine.

Taking her hand, I lead her into the steamy shower. The water cascades down on us, washing away any lingering doubts or fears. We embrace the warmth of the water enveloping us as we share a passionate kiss.

I can feel her trembling in my arms, the delicate vibrations of her body mirroring the turmoil of emotions coursing through me. I want to protect her, to be her safe haven, but at the same time, I can't deny the ravenous hunger that consumes me for her.

I pull away slightly, my eyes searching hers, seeking permission to unleash the desires that have been building within me. She nods, her eyes filled with trust and love. I run my hands down her waist, feeling the curve of her hips as she wraps her legs around me.

I lift her, and as she wraps her legs around my waist, she lets out a soft moan that only fuels the fire within me. Carrying her, I walk us back towards the bed. The water from the shower runs down our bodies as we make our way.

I lay her down on the soft, luxurious linens, her eyes never leaving mine. With a gentle smile, I lower my head and trail kisses down her body, her skin glistening from the water droplets. I savor each touch, each taste, as I worship her with my lips, letting her know just how much I adore her. Slowly, I make my way to her most sensitive spots, my tongue tracing patterns and teasing her into breathless moans. I glance up and see her eyes closed.

"Open your eyes, and don't take them off me," I command. Her eyes snap open and I am lost in the sea of desire in them. I take her swollen clit between my lips and suckle while I insert one finger into her tight passage.

"Oh, Giovanni," she cries.

My lips curl into a predatory grin as I suck harder, causing her to gasp and arch her back. My fingers plunge deeper into her, scissoring and stretching her tight passage as I prepare to claim her virginity. I am not known for being gentle, but with her, I want to ease her into the inevitable pain. As I push in and out, my fingers grow slick with her desire, marking her as mine before I even take her body.

"Giovanni, I need," she moans. "I need, I need."

I thrust my fingers into her with an unrelenting force, feeling the walls of her tightness gripping and pulling me deeper. The sounds of her moans and cries fill the air as I increase my speed, determined to push her to the brink. Her body writhes beneath mine as I feel her pussy clench around me, signaling her impending release. With a swift motion, I yank my fingers out and clamp down on her swollen clit, eliciting a primal scream from deep within her. Her body convulses in ecstasy as I continue to stroke and tease her sensitive nub, drawing out every last drop of pleasure from her quivering form.

As I feel her body tremble and arch beneath me, I know she's on the edge, ready for the fulfillment of our desires. I guide myself to her opening.

"You are mine," I say, my voice ragged with desire. With

one power thrust, I push in, breaking her virginal barrier. Angelina cries out in pain and tries to pull away. I grasp her hips to hold her in place.

And I hold her, my body pressing hard against hers, both of us trembling with a mixture of agony and tension. The moment may have been rough, but it was necessary. I start to move inside her slowly, taking care not to hurt her. As I do, her cries of pain slowly transform into cries of pleasure, mingling with her soft moans.

The pleasure builds and builds, and soon Angelina's eyes roll back into her head, tension filling her body as she reaches her peak. I feel her body convulse, the walls of her pussy tightening around me, pulling me deeper inside. Angelina wraps her legs around me, pulling me even closer in her ecstasy.

As the waves of pleasure wash over us, I slow my thrusts, savoring the feeling of being inside her, knowing that I will be there forever. I pull from her and smile at the blood streaking my cock. The mixture of our cum pour out of her, tinted red from her broken virginity. The stark white sheet was stained with the proof of her purity. Angelina was mine, and I would never let anyone come between us.

What the fuck was I doing? I couldn't stop caressing Angelina's smooth skin. I was already addicted to the crackling energy that followed between us whenever we touched.

As a naive fifteen-year-old virgin, I eagerly gave in to my twenty-year-old nanny's seduction in my childhood bed. The moment my dick sank into her wet pussy was when my inner dragon finally broke free from its cage, unleashing a wave of primal sexual rage I had never known was possible. Even though it was my first time, I fucked her like I had been doing it for years.

From a young age, my father advised me about the beast that lived inside every man in our family. Drago, as he called it, would lie dormant until provoked by anger or desire. As I grew older, I learned to control and unleash this rage in order to protect my family and The Famiglia. But now, I question if it's truly worth the cost of living with such an unpredictable monster inside of me. Am I just a pawn in this legacy of violence?

He was like a wild animal, rattling his cage in desperation as I crawled between Angelina's legs. He demanded to be set free, and for one fleeting moment, I did. But instead of taking things slowly and allowing her to adjust, he rammed into her with primal force, claiming her body as if it were his right. The sound of flesh slapping against flesh echoed through the room as their bodies became one, consumed by raw desire.

"Giovanni, are you okay?" she asks, her hand stroking the hair on my chest.

Was I? Not really, but I couldn't bring myself to admit the truth. After all, a man like me couldn't show weakness. So, I simply grunt in response and pull her closer to me. I need her. I want her. And for now, I want to bask in the afterglow of our first time together.

As I held her tight, I couldn't help but wonder what had led to this moment. Had it been fate that I was the one who met with Charles or something even bigger? I should have said no to his request. Angelina was too pure for me and so delicate for Drago.

In my baser desires, Angelina was just like any other woman I had been with. However, my soul knew she was different. When I invoked the rite, I thought I could control Drago. I was going to give Angelina at least a normal wedding night without the influence of The Famiglia. However, my plans were shattered, my control slipping through my fingers like sand. Every fiber of my being screamed for me to stop, but it was too late. His wild energy had been unleashed, and I could see the fear in her eyes, a primal terror that sent shivers down my spine. I had lost all power, and she was at his mercy. Thankfully, I was able to gain control and lock him back up, but it was too late. I had hurt her even worse than Morgan had.

"Hey," Angelina says, leaning up and looking into my eyes. God, she is so beautiful. "Talk to me."

My shame of what I had done weighed me down. Never in my life had I said what I wanted to tell her.

"Angelina," I whispered, my voice barely more than a

whisper. "I'm sorry. I lost control, and I hurt you." I trailed off, unable to find the words to describe the beast that drank from my soul.

I could see the uncertainty in her eyes, but there was also understanding and concern. She reached up and cupped my face in her hands, her eyes searching mine. "It's okay."

I close my eyes and drink in the warmth of her hands. Her calming energy sinks deep down to Drago, who hums with contentment. Never in my life had he been so calm.

I open my eyes and give her a small smile. "Let me run you a bath. It will help with the soreness."

A soft blush rises to her cheeks, causing them to glow with a rosy hue. She brings her lower lip between her teeth, a subtle but sensual gesture that only adds to her shyness. The way she hides behind her locks of hair and avoids direct eye contact is undeniably alluring. It's as if she holds a secret within herself, just waiting to be discovered. And at that moment, her shyness becomes the most enticing thing about her.

I gently kiss her lips before getting out of bed and slipping on a pair of sleep pants. I walk into the bathroom, turn on the tap, and adjust the water temperature to my liking. Reaching for a bottle on the shelf, I pour a generous amount of bubble bath under the flow. The sweet aroma fills the room as bubbles begin to form in the tub.

I go back in the room to find Angelina sitting on the side of the bed, looking down at the blood stain on the white sheets. My heart thunders in my chest. I come to her side and brush my hand down her arm. "Come. I'll take care of this while you soak."

She turns her face up to me. "I should do it."

"No, it is my duty. Now, come before I turn you over my knee for not obeying," I say, giving her a wink.

She stands and takes my hand. I lead her into the bathroom and help her into the tub. "Oh, it's hot," she says, sinking.

"Lean back and let it do its work," I say, placing a thick towel behind her neck. She sighs deeply and closes her eyes.

"God, this feels heavenly," she moans.

Fuck me, she is a sexy sight, and hearing her moans causes my cock to twitch. However, I need to take care of a few things. I turn on the sound system, and the room is bathed in the sultry sounds of smooth jazz. Angelina told me it was her favorite. "I'll be right back."

I walk out of the room and pull the sheets from the bed. Carrying them to the bedroom door, I quietly open it to find my fellow brothers-in-crime standing with shit-eating grins on their faces.

"Never pegged her as a screamer," Luca says.

"Fuck you, asshole," I say, handing over the sheets.

The rite promised us the chance to share our first time alone without prying eyes or judgmental whispers. But the sheets had to be carefully sealed and locked away in a secret box within The Commission's walls. They would serve as irrefutable proof of Angelina's purity if anyone dared to question it.

"Move out of the way, you juvenile delinquents," Margaret says, pushing Davide and Danti out of the way. "I'll take care of making the bed and cleaning up dinner."

"Thank you."

She touches my arm and smiles at me. "It is my pleasure. I can't wait to get to know Mrs. Genovese."

She walks in and quietly begins to work. I turn back to the guys. "Thanks for doing this for me."

"Gio, we will always have your back like you have ours. Now, go make your wife scream some more," Luca says, wiggling his eyebrows.

"Just you wait, you asshole. One day, you will find some

lost soul who will have pity on you and marry you," I say, punching him in the shoulder. "Now get out."

They turn and walk down the hall, laughing and joking as they go. I couldn't ask for better friends.

I walk back into the bedroom to see Margaret finishing up the bed. I was thankful for her tireless service all these years. She had been with the Genovese family since I was a baby. When my mother passed away from cancer, Margaret stepped in as the motherly figure when I needed one.

I step over and place my hand on hers. "Thank you for everything." She gives me one of her warm smiles and a nod. I know she is trying to be quiet, not wanting Angelina to feel embarrassed.

As I step back into the bathroom, the calming warmth of the tub beckons me. Angelina is submerged to her neck, her eyes closed, and a small smile graces her lips.

"Hey, Angelina," I start, my voice barely above a whisper.

Her eyes open, and she looks up at me. "Hey," she says, her voice gentle and soothing.

I am still wrestling with the thought that she is my wife. She is too good for me, but there was no way in hell I was giving her up.

"Move forward," I command as I slip my pants off my cock bounces as it is freed from its confinement. She looks at it and licks her lips which causes me to even become harder.

"Okay," she whispers, her eyes locked on my naked erection. I can see desire and curiosity.

Slowly, she slides forward, and I climb in stinking into the warm water. I wrap my arm around her waist and pull her back. Her fingertips lightly touch my thigh, sending a jolt of pleasure down below.

"Angelina," I warn as Drago begins to become restless. My heart is racing, and my cock is throbbing with need. I don't want to hurt her, but I need her. I need to feel her heat and softness around me. I reach down and begin stroking her lips.

"Giovanni," she moans.

It feels like an eternity before I can bear it any longer. My heart is thundering in my chest, and my cock is aching with desire. I know I need to treasure this moment, but the need to possess her, to feel her skin beneath mine, is too overwhelming.

I grip her hips and pull her closer as I lower her pussy onto my straining cock.

Oh, God. She is tight and hot. I can feel her inner muscles gripping me, sending waves of pleasure coursing through my body.

I begin to thrust, and her moans fill the room, mingling perfectly with the smooth jazz that plays in the background. Water splashes around us as we find our rhythm, the warm, sudsy water enveloping our bodies, creating a sensual cocoon. My hands grip her hips, lift her, and turn her so we are facing. I need to see her face as she comes. I push back into her in one slow, deliberate thrust, relishing the feeling of her tight channel.

Her nails dig into my shoulders as she arches her back, pulling me deeper inside her.

I watch her face as her eyes close, her lips part, her breath coming in short gasps. She is lost in the moment, surrendering to the pleasure and the sensations, and it fills me with a strange combination of pride and protectiveness.

"You're mine," I growl, my voice rough with emotion. "I am the one who will keep you safe, cherish you, and give you pleasure beyond your wildest dreams."

She moans again, her body writhing beneath me. I pick up the pace, my thrusts becoming harder and faster. The water around us churns, bubbles rising to the surface like a testament to the intense passion we share.

Our bodies move in perfect sync, and soon, I feel her muscles tighten around me, her inner walls clinging to me like a vise. She lets out a high-pitched cry as she arches her back, her head thrown back and her eyes wide open. I can see the sheer pleasure written all over her face.

Her climax pulls me over the edge too, and I thrust into her one final time, my cock throbbing and releasing deep inside her. I keep my eyes on her face, drinking in her expression of pure ecstasy.

We stay like that for a few minutes, our bodies still connected, the water around us muffled. I exhale deeply and rest my forehead against hers. She strokes my hair, and I know she is trying to comfort me as well.

I don't know what is happening to me, but whatever it is, I am ready for it.

Chapter Twenty-Seven

ANGELINA

I can't believe it has been two months since my wedding. Giovanni and I are still getting to know each other. Most of the time, we can't keep our hands off each other. However, there have been times when I wanted to scream at the top of my lungs.

Even though I grew up never leaving my house, I still had freedom. If I wanted to stay up half the night painting, then I did. Giovanni threw a fit when he caught me painting in my studio at three in the morning. He was so pissed he padlocked the door for a week and gave me my first punishment.

After locking the door, he took me to his office.

"Angelina, you are to never be up that late again," he growled.

"I didn't realize it was that late. The room doesn't have a clock."

"And where was your phone?" he asks.

It was then I remembered I had left it on the nightstand when I got up. Giovanni was sleeping so peacefully, and I couldn't sleep because my creative urges were going wild.

I look down at my feet, suddenly feeling like a naughty child being scolded. "I'm sorry, Giovanni," I mumble, not daring to meet his gaze.

His expression softens slightly, but his tone remains firm. "This behavior is unacceptable, Angelina. You need to remember that you are now a part of my life, and that means there are rules you must abide by."

I nod, trying to suppress the frustration welling inside me. In the beginning, our marriage felt like a whirlwind fairytale romance. But as time went on, I realized there were aspects of being Giovanni's wife that were suffocating me.

He continued, his voice growing quieter yet no less intense. "You are not a prisoner here, Angelina. But you need to understand that your actions have consequences. I locked your studio for a week because I want you to take this seriously."

A pang of resentment surged through me at his words. How could I let myself be treated like a child? How could I allow my passion and creativity to be locked away? These were the questions that resounded in my mind as I stood before Giovanni, my eyes burning with a mixture of anger and defeat.

"I understand, Giovanni," I said, my voice steady but tinged with a hint of defiance. "But you have to understand that painting is not just a hobby for me. It's a part of who I am. Locking away my studio feels like you're locking away a part of me."

He sighed, his features softening as he looked into my eyes. "Angelina, I didn't mean to stifle your creativity. I just worry about you. The late nights, the lack of sleep... it concerns me. I want you to be healthy and take care of yourself."

A wave of guilt washed over me, mingling with the resentment. He did care about me. There was no doubt about that.

"I told you that I am the head of this household. My rules are the law. You will do as I say. Seeing it is your first punishment as my wife, I will be giving you twenty smacks on your bare ass for putting your health in jeopardy."

"Do what?" I ask. He wasn't serious about this, was he?

He sat down in a chair and motioned for me to come over. I walked over, and he pulled me across his lap. I squealed at the motion. He pulled my dress up and my panties down. "Don't cover your ass, or I will tie your hand together. Do you understand?"

"Giovanni, don't do this," I begged. Never in my life had my father ever spanked me. Now, my husband was, and that was just wrong.

"Oh my god, is he about to spank me?" I thought to myself, my heart racing. How can I make him understand I'm not like a child? I'm a grown woman, and I should be able to make my own decisions about how I spend my time.

But as he raised his hand and brought it down on my bare bottom, the pain was like nothing I'd ever experienced. I couldn't help but cry out, my body convulsing under the force of it all.

"This is what happens when you break the rules, Angelina," he said, his voice firm. "This is what happens when you don't listen and don't respect the rules of our household."

Tears streaming down my face, I felt so powerless and humiliated. How could this be happening? This wasn't the marriage I had envisioned, the life of passion and adventure I had hoped for. Instead, I found myself in a situation where I was constantly struggling for control.

As the spanking continued, my protests turned into sobs, and soon, I was begging him to stop. But he doesn't. He continued to spank me until I was sure I couldn't take it anymore. Finally, when he was done, he lifted me and held me close, his voice gentle as he spoke.

"Angelina, I know this is hard for you. But I only want what's best for you. I need you to understand that these rules are for your own good. They are to help you stay safe, healthy, and happy."

Tears streaming down my face, I found myself nodding in agreement. Despite my humiliation, I could see that Giovanni was genuinely concerned about my well-being. I just needed time to adjust to this new way of life.

With tears still in my eyes, I whispered, "I understand, Giovanni. I will try to abide by your rules and respect our household. No more late-night painting sessions for me."

He nodded, a small smile appearing on his face. "That's good, Angelina. I'm proud of you for taking responsibility for your actions and for agreeing to change your behavior. However, if you ever break the rules again, understand that there will be consequences."

I took a deep breath, feeling a sense of relief wash over me. I could see that Giovanni truly loved me and wanted the best for me. It was up to me to make this marriage work, even if it meant making some sacrifices and adjustments along the way.

As I left his office, I couldn't shake off the feeling of humiliation and powerlessness that still lingered within me. But as I walked back to my room and stared at the clock on the wall, I realized that Giovanni was right. I needed to take things slower and be more aware of my actions, especially as a new wife.

In the following weeks, I made sure to follow Giovanni's rules and tried to understand his perspective on things. I still missed the late-night painting sessions, but I found other ways to channel my creativity and passion. I started exploring the grounds of our estate and discovered the beauty of nature surrounding our home. I also began reading more books and learning about new things that interested me.

When Giovanni unlocked my studio door, I was ready to add it to my life, not let it be my life. When I went into the studio, I put on a timer so I wouldn't get lost in my creativity and break Giovanni's rule.

"Angelina," Giovanni calls out as he walks in the front door.

"In here," I say, happy to know he was home.

In a matter of seconds, he appears around the corner with a look of grave concern etched on his face. In one swift motion, I leap to my feet and sprint towards him. He engulfs me in his massive arms, squeezing me tightly against his chest. The thunderous beats of his heart reverberate through my body. "What is it?"

He pulls back and strokes the side of my face. "Do you know I will do anything I can to keep you safe?"

"Yes," I say. His words were to comfort me but they instead caused me to worry.

"The trial date has been set for Peter Morgan," he says, his eyes never leaving mine.

"When?" I ask as I fist my hands on his suit jacket. For weeks after the attack, I woke up with nightmares of Peter. Each was as terrifying as the attack itself. If Giovanni hadn't broken into the room when he did, I was sure Peter would have raped me.

I remember the night vividly, and I shuddered at the thought of it. "When is the trial?" I ask again, my voice barely above a whisper.

Giovanni's expression softens, and he takes my hands in his. "The trial is set for two days from today."

The air sucked out of the room. I couldn't believe it. After all this time, we were finally going to get justice for what Peter did to me. I couldn't help but feel a sense of relief wash over me. It had been a long and dark journey, but I knew that this was a step in the right direction.

I knew the next two days would be challenging, but I was ready for the fight. I was prepared to stand up to Peter and ensure he couldn't hurt anyone else. I was ready to move on with my life and help serve justice to the man who had tried to take that away from me.

Unlike the typical judicial system, The Famiglia was governed by The Commission. Peter himself had been on The Commission, which made this trial even more precarious. Then, to add to that, he attacked me, who was going to be married to a founding son. Giovanni was on The Commission. However, he wasn't allowed to cast a vote.

Giovanni's voice dripped with chilling confidence as he assured me that Peter Morgan would be found guilty beyond a shadow of a doubt. I could feel the weight of all the damning evidence against him and my testimony, a heavy burden that would surely lead to the most severe punishment. Giovanni refused to disclose what that punishment would be, but in my heart, I knew it had to be something unimaginably cruel. As long as it meant I was safe from Peter's revenge, I didn't want to know the details. The thought of him coming after me filled me with unspeakable terror, and I was willing to do whatever it took to ensure he stayed far away from me forever.

My stomach churns, and bile rises in my throat as I stand in front of the bathroom mirror. The thought of seeing Peter Morgan makes me want to vomit, my nerves raw from the horrific memories of his attack. For the past two nights, I've woken up screaming, my body drenched in sweat as I relive every excruciating detail. Giovanni's strong arms wrap around me, but even his comforting embrace cannot ease the terror that grips me at the thought of facing Peter again. He may have physically hurt me, but the emotional scars he left behind are just as agonizingly painful.

"Angelina," Giovanni says as he wraps his arm around my waist. "It is time to leave."

I desperately squeeze my eyes shut, willing myself to hold back the flood of emotions threatening to overwhelm me. I don't want to break down, but the weight of everything weighing on me is almost unbearable.

"I don't think I can do this," I whisper.

He turns me and lifts my face. "You are Angelina Genovese, wife of a founding son. You are stronger than anyone I have ever known, and I'm proud to call you my wife. You can do this and will do so with your head held high. Now let us get this day over with so we can come home, and I can fuck you all night long," he says in a voice gravely with sex appeal.

"Fuck me," I groan, my panties drenched.

He gives me a wink and a crooked smile. "Later, I promise."

Chapter Twenty-Eight

It is taking everything I have not to rush the fucking asshole and break his neck.

Angelina and I arrive at the compound, and I am shocked to see how many members donning their black cloaks were there. All the members of The Famiglia were notified of the case against Peter Morgan because of his station in The Commission. After today's trial, the members will hold an election to elect the consigliere, who will be taking Peter's place. It was a prestigious position with power and wealth. The position was for life, or if he broke a law of The Famiglia.

Members of The Famiglia received a stipend from the profits of the many businesses and stocks The Famiglia owned. The consigliere received an extra stipend for the service to The Famiglia.

We pull up in front of The Commission building, and I see four red-cloaked men, and someone cloaked in black. I couldn't see their faces or even see the crests on their red cloaks to know who they were. Davide, Danti, Luca, and Andrea were waiting for us. They weren't here for The Commission. They were here for me and Angelina. We are my brothers not by blood but by devotion. The man in black could only be one person, Charles. Since the wedding, he had given Angelina and me the room to get to know each other better. I knew he called a couple of times a week to talk to her. We had gone out to dinner with him twice. The first time, he was nervous, looking around for any possible threats. I knew he didn't think I could protect her. However, he had been looking over his shoulder for over twenty-five years, wondering when The Corporation or the Cuban mafia made their move. Just because it had been twenty-one since their last attack didn't mean they were gone for good. Knowing this, I increased security not only for Angelina but also for Charles. Neither one of them knew just how much.

I got out of the car, pulled the hood of my cloak over my head, and surveyed the area for any threats. I knew it was almost impossible, but I wouldn't take any by chance. Angelina was too important to allow anything to happen to her. When I felt all was safe, I assisted Angelina from the car, her black cloak covering every inch of her.

Charles stepped forward. "Hey, baby girl."

Angelina gasped. "Daddy? What are you doing here?"

"Do you really think I wouldn't be here to support you?" he said, pulling her into his arms.

She pulls away. "You are going to hear some horrible things in there."

"I know, but you didn't do anything wrong. This is all on the asshole who laid a hand on you. I am so proud of you," Charles says.

"Charles, we need to get inside," I say.

"Of course," he replies.

I take Angelina's hand, and we walk toward the door. Hamm and Davide walk in front of us while the rest of my brothers protect us from the rear.

I navigate us through the labyrinthine halls, each turn and twist purposely designed to disorient intruders. The walls seem to shift and morph, a maze of endless corridors that threaten to swallow anyone who was not of The Famiglia.

We finally arrive at the door of the courtroom. I took a deep breath before pushing open the door. The rest of The Commission are seated at a massive table position above the ground. It was designed to give the appearance of power and superiority.

Over the years, I had sat with them and passed judgment on those members who foolishly thought they could break our laws without punishment. From the position of the high table, the guilty looked tiny and vulnerable to The Commission's wrath.

Davide, Danti, Luca, and Andrea take their seats at the high table with the three consigliere. It was made to seat the nine men of The Commission. Never in the history of The Famiglia had The Commission held a trial where two members were absent from their seats. I wasn't allowed at the table since I was the wrong party and one of the consiglieri was the one on trial. The men still alive who helped Peter during the attack would be brought to trial after Peter's judgment.

Gripping Angelina's hand tightly, I lead her into the prosecution's area. Dr. Bianchi is already sitting in the area, flanked by my security team, who witnessed Peter's heinous actions. I carefully remove Angelina's hood, revealing her trembling form with an even paler complexion than before. Taking my seat next to her, I can feel the weight of the room bearing down on us as we prepare to face our enemy.

My heart races as I survey the packed gallery, filled with eager faces hungry for every gory detail of what happened to Angelina. These vultures aren't here for justice. They want to revel in my failure to protect my future bride.

The door on the far left opens. Four guards usher in Peter Morgan. His face was gaunt and sunken, his skin sallow and pale from his time in Tartarus, the prison of The Famiglia.

The ominous name of Tarartus sent shivers down the spines of those who knew of its existence. Hidden deep within The Commission building was a labyrinth of limestone tunnels and chambers, serving as The Famiglia's ultimate punishment for those who dared to break their laws. The air inside was thick with the stench of death and decay, the remains of those who had met their fate within its confines. Torches burned low, casting eerie shadows along the walls, and the sound of dripping water echoed through the dark corridors. It was a place that struck fear into even the bravest members of The Famiglia, a constant reminder of what could happen if one strayed from their strict code of conduct.

Peter glances towards me, and his lips break out with a sinister smile. He then looks at Angelina. The asshole undresses her with his eyes. His tongue comes out, and he licks his lips.

A surge of uncontrollable rage washes over me, a sensation unlike anything I had ever experienced before. My inner dragon, caged and restrained for so long, finally breaks free. My body trembles with the intensity of the emotion as I open the gate to unleash its fury. The raw power and energy pulsate through me like an unstoppable force, consuming all rational thought and control. At this moment, I welcome his release, surrendering to my primal instincts.

I leap to my feet and charge toward Peter. As I close in on Peter, I can feel the energy surging through my body, fueling my every movement. The consigliere and other members of The Famiglia were on their feet, staring at me in disbelief and horror. But I didn't care. All that mattered was protecting Angelina and avenging what happened to her.

I tackle Peter to the cold, hard floor of the courtroom. His eyes widen in fear as I pin him down, my hands around his throat. The sound of his struggling breath echoes in my ears as I bare my teeth, snarling at him like a caged animal.

"You're never going to hurt her again," I growl, my voice

shaking with fury. "You've seen what I'm capable of. You'll regret ever laying a hand on her."

Peter chokes and grasps at my arm in desperation. "I didn't ask for this! They made me."

I sneer as I lean closer, my voice a low, threatening growl. "Too late. You've done the unforgivable. Now, you pay."

With that, I tighten my grip around his throat, feeling the satisfying pressure of his windpipe. His eyes bulge, gasping for air.

I see the lights of life leaving his eyes as I feel arms coming around me. I fight against Davide, Danti, Luca, and Andrea, their expressions a mix of fury and protectiveness. They grab me, their hands on my arms, trying to pry my hands off Peter's neck.

"What are you doing?" demands Davide. "This is not our way!"

"He hurt her," I growl, fighting against his hold.

"He did and will be punished, but Giovanni, you can't do it. You invoked the rite," Luca says, touching my shoulder.

I look up, and the red haze of fury clears.

"No. I will not let him hurt her again," I spat, struggling.

Andrea steps forward. "It's not about what you want. It's about what's best for Angelina, the Famiglia, and our honor. You're crossing the line between protector and vigilant."

"This is not about what's best for the Famiglia," I grind out through clenched teeth. "This is about avenging what he did to her."

"For now," Danti agrees, "but what happens when you start to cross the line between justice and vengeance? You'll lose control, just like Peter did. That's an enemy we cannot afford to have."

I pause, my chest heaving as I try to catch my breath, my anger slowly fading under the weight of their words. I let out a shaky sigh.

"I understand," I say, reluctant acceptance in my voice.

"But I'll never forgive him. I'll never forget what he did to her."

"I know, Giovanni," Davide replies, his voice soothing and understanding. "But for now, we must follow The Famiglia's law and code. Peter's punishment will come, but The Commission will decide it. Let them decide his fate, not you."

Danti nods in agreement. "You know the consequences of breaking the law. You've seen what happens to those who cross the line. We cannot let our emotions cloud our judgment."

Luca places a hand on my shoulder, his gaze firm but compassionate. "You've done enough, Giovanni. You've protected Angelina and shown Peter the consequences of his actions. Now, let us handle the rest."

I take a deep breath, feeling the tension leaving my body. I look at Angelina, her eyes wide with fear, and give her a reas-suring nod. Without another look at Peter, I return to Angelina and pull her into my arms. "I'll let them handle this, but know I will always protect you."

"I know you will," she murmurs into my chest.

The trial continues, and Angelina shows the epitome of strength and dignity as she tells what happened. I am amazed and so fucking proud of her.

After all the testimony, The Commission goes into cham-bers to discuss the outcome. Peter is escorted out of the room to wait for the decision. Once he left, Angelina let out a sigh of relief.

"Are you okay?" I ask.

"Yes. I just hope they don't let him go. I don't know if I could go out if I thought he would be around the next corner," she admits.

I vow to take justice into my own hands if The Famiglia fails to punish him appropriately. He will never lay a finger on my beloved wife again. But deep down, I pray it won't come to that. My brothers hold the power of four votes on The Commission, and I know they would not hesitate to vote for the most severe punishment possible. Nothing less than death would satisfy their thirst for revenge.

The chamber door opens, and The Commission returns to their seats. I look at the faces of my brothers, trying to read the decision. I can read just about anybody's thoughts except them.

"Bring back the accused," Davide boomed.

My eyes shift to the door, and seconds later, it opens. The Famiglia guard brings Peter back to the courtroom. Unlike the last time, he doesn't look my way.

"Peter Morgan, The Commission has found you guilty on all counts. You have brought disgrace to not only The Famiglia but to The Commission. Your betrayal of your oath as consigliere dictates the punishment to be imposed. Immediate death by hanging," Davide says without any emotions. "Take him to the gallows."

Peter hangs his head as the guard leads him from the room. I am required to witness his hanging. However, Angelina did not. I glanced around and found Charles. I motion for him to come to us. He makes his way over.

"Charles, could you take Angelina back to our estate? I must do a few things before I can leave," I say.

"I don't want to leave without you," Angelina cries, gripping my hand.

"I know, my love, but I have to do this. I've already crossed one line. I won't cross another. We've done enough. Let The Famiglia handle this now."

Tears well up in her eyes, and I can see the fear and anxiety etched on her face. But I know I have to be strong for her. This was the reality of our life, and I had to show her that I could control my emotions and make the right decisions, even if it hurt to do so.

"I'll be back as soon as possible," I promise, giving her one last kiss before Charles leads her away.

My heart races as I join Davide, Luca, Andrea, and Danti.

We exit The Commission building and move swiftly through the dimly lit passageway where the gallows looms menacingly. The Famiglia guard drags Peter up the steps, a noose already fixed tightly around his neck. The crowd falls silent, their anticipation palpable as they wait for the trapdoor to drop. But Peter's head rises defiantly, his eyes locking with mine, fear etched across his face, begging for mercy that will never come.

The bell chimes, and the door drops. The guilty pays for his crimes.

ocean breeze still lingered on our clothes, and I could almost taste the salt on my lips as I sat at my easel and mixed vibrant hues onto my canvas. The memories of lazy days spent lounging on white sandy beaches and exploring hidden coves flooded my mind, fueling my creativity. Each brushstroke was infused with the warmth of our love and the serenity of our special time together. As I worked, the sounds of seagulls and crashing waves echoed in my ears, transporting me back to our idyllic getaway.

After being consumed by my art in the past, I learned to set boundaries. With each brush stroke, I released all my emotions onto the canvas with a renewed zeal. The vibrant hues of the Mediterranean danced across the surface as if infused with a magical energy. Bursts of fiery orange and yellow punctuated the deep blues of the sea, and hints of lush greenery peeked through the warm tones. My entire being was immersed in this world of color and expression.

My phone rings, and for a moment, I think it is my alarm, but as it sounds for a second time, I realize it is my phone ringing. I rush to pick it up, dropping the paintbrush onto my pallet.

"Hello," I say.

"Angelina, it's Lucy."

"Lucy, hello. How are you?" I ask, excited to be hearing from her. She was my age, and I enjoyed the time we spent together before the wedding. I never had a friend growing up.

"Doing great. I was wondering if you would like to go to lunch and do some shopping afterward. A formal event is coming up at The Famiglia compound, and I need to find something," she asks.

"That sounds nice. Let me ask Giovanni, and I will get back to you."

She pauses for a moment. "I see you are fitting in well to the ways of The Famiglia. If Giovanni asks, which I know he will, Luca knows and has given his permission."

"Oh, I didn't know you had the same rules I did," I say.

Lucy chuckles on the other end of the line. "Oh, Angelina, it's not just you. The rules apply to all of us. Until we are married, we must obey the rules of our fathers and brothers."

"I guess I am still learning. Talk to you soon." I hang up with Lucy and make my way to find Giovanni.

I find him in his study, surrounded by stacks of papers spread out on his desk. His eyes flicker with concentration as he studies the document in front of him. The sight of him engrossed in his work tugs at my heartstrings, reminding me of how much he sacrifices for The Famiglia.

"Giovanni," I say softly, entering the room.

He looks up from his papers, a smile lighting up his face as he sees me. "Angelina," he replies, his voice filled with warmth and affection. "What brings you here?"

"I just received a call from Lucy," I say, walking closer to him. "She invited me for lunch and shopping. Supposedly, there's a formal event tomorrow at The Famiglia compound, and she needs to find something."

Giovanni leans back in his chair, his eyes locked onto mine. "And what does Lucy need to find that requires your presence?"

I feel a flutter of nervousness in my stomach, unsure of how he will react to me spending time with one of the other women in The Famiglia. "She just wants some company," I say, trying to keep my voice steady. "And Luca has given his permission."

Giovanni's expression softens, and he runs a hand through his dark hair. "I see," he says, his tone thoughtful. "Well, if Luca has given his permission, I trust his judgment. I have been so busy with my research that I had forgotten about the event. You know I pick out all your clothing?"

"Yes, sir," I say, lowering my eyes.

I hear the scrape of his chair as he pulls me forcefully between his legs. His massive hands hungrily trace a path up my trembling thighs until they reach the thin barrier of my panties. His touch is electric, sending shivers down my spine as he grips and pulls at the fabric, his desire for me evident in every movement. He brushes his thumb over my aching clit. "Every inch of you belongs to me."

"Yes, sir," I moan, leaning my hips back against the desk and spreading my legs.

He growls, and in one swift motion, he pushes all the papers off the desk and sits me on it. "Put your feet on the desk and lean back," he demands.

I quickly do as he asks. He grasps the sides of the panties and tears them off. The cool air of the room hits my sensitive pussy. He then takes my ankles in his strong hands, raising my legs to rest on his broad shoulders.

"How much do you trust me, Angelina?" he asks, his eyes never leaving mine.

"I trust you completely, Giovanni," I reply, my voice trembling slightly.

"Then trust me in this," he says, positioning himself at my entrance.

I feel the tip of his hard cock pressing against my entrance, and I can't help but moan. He slides in slowly, stretching me wide as he enters me. I gasp at the sensation of fullness and the pleasure it brings.

"God, you feel so good, Angelina," he murmurs, his deep voice sending shivers down my spine.

He begins to thrust, each movement sending waves of pleasure through me. My hands grip the edge of the desk, my nails digging into the wood as I claw my way into the pleasure. Giovanni's strong arms hold me tight, his grip on my thighs never wavering as he continues to pound into me. His eyes never leave mine, his expression a mix of love and lust.

As the waves of pleasure build, I can feel myself growing closer to the edge. Giovanni's pace quickens, his thrusts becoming more urgent. I can feel his cock throbbing inside me, and I know that he's close too.

"Harder, Giovanni," I beg, arching my back to meet his thrusts. "I need more."

He didn't hesitate as his thrusts became even more powerful. The sound of our bodies slapping together fills the room. I'm so close, the tension in my body building with each thrust.

Finally, I can't take it any longer. I let out a loud cry as I come.

His body presses against mine with such force that the desk shudders beneath us. I moan in ecstasy as he groans, "Yes!" and thrust into me with primal urgency. I could feel every inch of him inside me, filling me up as he emptied himself deep within my core. He collapses on top of me, his ragged breaths mingling with mine in a tangle of bodies and desires. The room is filled with the scent of sex and sweat.

I run my hand through his hair and sigh with contentment. I love this man so fucking much. The words are on the tip of my tongue. However, I can't say them.

Giovanni raises, and his cock slips out of me. Our combined hot cum pours from my opening and onto his desk.

"Damn, that is hot," he growls.

I feel my face burn with shame. "I'm sorry."

He places his hands on either side of my face and tilts it so I am looking straight into his eyes. "There is nothing to be sorry about. Seeing our cum pouring out of you is the sexiest thing I've ever witnessed."

"But your desk," I say, worried it had caused damage to his expensive desk. "It is ruined."

"Ruined? No fucking way. I'm never getting rid of this desk. Every time I sit here, I will remember this. I just hope the smell remains," he says, wagging his eyebrows. "Now, go put on the black and white Dior dress and the Jimmy Choo red mules. Enjoy lunch with Lucy, and go shopping for your gown for the event afterward."

"Really?" I ask.

"Yes. I just ask for you to video me with the ones you pick out," he says.

"I can do that. Thank you, Giovanni," I say.

"Make sure you don't stray away from Mattia."

"I promise."

"Good. Now go call Lucy and get ready. I've got to clean up this mess," he laughs.

I hesitantly lean in and place a fleeting kiss on his lips, unsure if he still feels the same. My words of love pour out as I gaze into his eyes, hoping he understands and doesn't shatter my heart with rejection.

"Oh, my God, I can't believe we got in here," Lucy exclaims as we pull up in front of Bella Luna.

After our little passion display on Giovanni's desk, he asked if I wanted to go to Bella Luna for lunch. I knew it was one of his restaurants, and he wanted a place where he could control the security. Every action of his dominance gave me hope that he cared more than he said.

"Giovanni owns it, and we have a reserved table," I explain.

"How did I not know that Giovanni owned Bella Luna?" Lucy asks.

"I am always surprised at how many legal businesses my husband owns."

"Yeah, so does my family. Got to have something to offset all the illegal shit they do," Lucy says with a wink.

With our security around us, we walk into the entrance and wait for the hostess to acknowledge us. She looks up and turns back as if we weren't even here. What the fuck? Lucy gives me a questioning look. Did this woman not know who I was? I wait a few more moments before something deep inside comes alive. Burning Rage. Never in my life had I ever lost my temper. I've always been sweet and kind. However, this bitch is pushing me to the breaking point.

I clear my throat, hoping she will say something, but she doesn't. Breathing in my nose and out of my mouth, I try to calm down. The door opens, and two men walk in, dressed in tailored suits.

"Jason, Richard, so good to see you again," the hostess says, walking around us and approaching the two men. "I have your table ready."

As they walk away, I feel the boiling rage inside me erupt like a volcano. Every ounce of self-control dissipates as I transform into Angelina Genovese - fierce, unstoppable. With determined steps, I charge towards her, meeting her in the center of the restaurant. This bitch is going down, and I will make sure she never forgets the name Angelina Genovese.

"Hey, you," I growl, reaching out and grabbing her arm.

She turns, and her mouth turns into a sneer. "What do you want?"

"I want to be seated," I bark.

"Well, we are booked. You need to make a reservation," she says.

I stand taller. "I don't need one."

"Oh, of course you do. This is a first-star establishment, not a fast-food restaurant," she snaps.

I twirl my hand around. "And who owes this first star establishment."

"Mr. Genovese," she says with a smile and starry look in her eyes. The bitch has the hots for my husband.

"Do you know who I am?" I ask.

"Someone who thinks she is important when she is not," she answers.

Lucy giggles beside me, and I can't help but smile. "Let me introduce myself. I am Angelina Genovese. I believe you want to know my husband on a more personal basis."

She huffs and pushes out her obvious fake tits. "Gio is not

married. I would know. We are very close," she says with a smirk.

"Really? Just how close?" I ask, playing along.

She leans towards me. "So close that I can still feel his dick inside me from this morning."

I couldn't help but break out in laughter. Reaching into my purse, I grab my phone and push Giovanni's number. He answers on the first ring.

"Angelina, is there something wrong?" he asks. I could hear the concern in his voice, and it warmed my heart.

"Gio, love, what is the manager's name here?"

"Why?" he asks.

I look at the hostess. "What is your name?"

"Jillian," she snaps.

"Jillian, the girl you had your dick in this morning doesn't believe I am your wife. I need to speak to the manager to clear this up so Lucy and I can have lunch," I say with a killer smile.

"Baby, you know that is a lie. I was in your pussy this morning," Giovanni says in a husky voice. "Stay where you are. Gibson will be there in a few seconds."

He hangs up. I look around, and I see the entire restaurant staring at us. I should feel self-conscious about it, but I don't. Giovanni would have done the same thing, only louder, if he were here.

"Mrs. Genovese."

As I turn, my gaze falls upon a strikingly handsome man. His broad shoulders and tall stature immediately capture my attention. His thick brown curls frame his chiseled jawline and rich brown eyes, making them stand out even more against his tanned skin. His fitted navy blue suit accentuates his muscular physique as if it were crafted specifically for him. The crisp lines and impeccable fit suggest luxury and sophistication.

"Yes. You must be Gibson," I say, holding out my hand.

"Yes, Mrs. Genovese," he says, shaking my hand. He turns

and looks at Jillian, whose mouth has fallen open. I bet she could blow a snowblower because it was so big.

"Jillian, go to my office now," Gibson barks.

"But, but, but," she stutters.

I close the distance between us and lean in close to her ear. I lace my voice with venom. "You've never experienced the sheer ecstasy of my husband's thick, long cock pounding deep inside you until you see stars. But I have. Three times this morning alone." My words drip with satisfaction as I taunt her with my sexual conquests.

I step back and smile up at Gibson. "We would like to be seated."

"Of course, Mrs. Genovese," Gibson says as he escorts us to our table.

We sit down and our waiter quickly takes our drink order. It is then I look around the room and catch the eyes of many women who give me a nod. I wonder how many times Jillian had treated other women like she treated me.

"I can't believe that happened," Lucy says.

"Me either. I've never lost my temper like that before."

"Well, you remind me of Giovanni when his dragon breaks out of his cage. Your eyes sparked with fire."

My phone rings, and when I pick it up, I smile. "Hello."

"Are you okay? Do you need me to come to you?" Giovanni asks, his voice full of concern. It makes me think he might care more than he lets on.

"I'm fine. We are at our table and waiting for our lunch."

"Mattia said you handled yourself so well that he didn't need to step in. I am so fucking proud of you," Giovanni purred. "Enjoy your lunch, and don't forget to send me the video."

"I will."

"You are in love with him," Lucy says.

"What?" I stutter.

She leans forward. "I am a daughter of The Famiglia, and

I know someday Luca will arrange a marriage with someone inside of the society. It won't be for love but for advantage. Seeing you with Giovanni makes me believe in love and how wonderful it can be," she says, her voice full of emotion.

"I love him," I confess.

"I can see that, and I am happy for you. You deserve it, Angelina," Lucy says, her eyes shining with unshed tears.

Reaching over, I place my hand over hers. "I sure you will." Her smile dissipates, and a look of sadness washes over her.

Our lunch comes, and we dig in. I learn so much about her and her family. We exchange our likes and dislikes and find we have very similar tastes. I couldn't help but grin over the fact I had made my first friend.

"**A**ngelina, you have to try on that one," Lucy squeals.

As I lift the dress from its hanger, my heart skips a beat. The deep midnight blue fabric shimmered in the light, adorned with delicate crystals that seemed to dance and twinkle with every movement. The corset bust was a work of art intricately adorned with tiny jewels and sparkling beads. The sheer fabric of the skirt cascaded down gracefully, revealing a daring slit on one side. The collar draped elegantly off my shoulders, held in place by a quilted band that added a touch of modernity to the ensemble. A matching quilted bow cinched at the waist completes the look with a touch of sophistication. It was undoubtedly one of the most breathtaking gowns I had ever seen.

"I am," I say, handing the dress to the saleslady who was helping us. Giovanni only gave me permission to buy a dress, but I also found several other outfits I wanted. They were in the dressing room as well, and I hoped he would allow me to get them. "I love several of the dresses you have selected as well."

"I know. It will be hard to decide," she says with a smile.

We go to the dressing rooms, a luxurious space with plush carpets and walls adorned with ornate mirrors. A three-way mirror stands against one wall, reflecting every angle of my appearance. The settee in the corner is made of soft velvet, its deep red color matching the rich tones of the room. I can almost see Giovanni lounging on it. His eyes fixed hungrily on me as I tried on each outfit.

I set my phone up on one of the ledges next to the mirror and hit video chat with Giovanni. He answers on the second ring, his chiseled jaw and piercing eyes boring into my soul.

"Hey, baby," he purrs, sending a jolt of need to my core.

"Hey."

"Did you find a dress?" he asks.

"Yes," I answer, biting my lip nervously.

"Angelina, what is it? I can tell you have something else you want to say."

"Are you sure you can't read minds?" I ask with a giggle.

"Maybe," he replies, giving me one of his crooked grins and a wink. Oh, my poor heart.

I look down at my phone. "Well, it's not just one dress. I found several outfits I wanted to try on."

"As long as I am the one taking them off you, go ahead," he says, his voice low and sultry.

I can't help but feel another jolt of desire between my legs, and I blush. "I have to try them on first, though," I remind him, my voice catching.

I see him sit back in his leather chair and bring a tumbler to his lips with the dark amber liquid I know is his favorite expensive bourbon. "Alright, let's start the show," he says in his husky voice, which stokes the fire in the pit of my stomach.

If he continues speaking like this, I would need to purchase new panties before I leave the store.

I remove my dress, placing it carefully on the bench. When I stand, Giovanni sucks in a breath. Glancing over my shoulder at the camera, I give him a cheeky grin. He didn't say anything, but the desire radiating from him was palpable.

"What is it?" I ask, my curiosity piqued.

"It's just you look so fucking amazing, Angelina," he says, his voice a ragged whisper.

"Thank you," I reply, my stomach flipping at his compliment.

I reach down and pick up the first dress, a simple yet stunning white number with spaghetti straps and a plunging neckline. As I hold it up, Giovanni's eyes lock on my chest.

"I want to see you in that," he says, his voice practically begging me.

I blush slightly but slip into the dress, the material falling effortlessly around me. I turn to show him the full view, and his eyes widen, his jaw hanging open. "I'm not sure if I want to fuck you or spank you," he adds with a chuckle.

I can't help but laugh at his words. I know that either would be an incredible turned-on, but right now, I just want him to understand that I'm in love with him. "I'll let you decide," I say, playfully biting my lip.

Slipping off the white dress, I try on the other outfits. Giovanni permits me to purchase all of them. Finally, I pick up the midnight blue gown. I take it off the hanger. As I step into the midnight blue gown, I can feel its delicate fabric shimmering against my skin, my heart beating wildly excitedly. I tug at the zipper, and when secure, I turn to the phone to see Giovanni's expression.

Instead of appreciating the dress, I see what looks like pure terror. As I open my mouth to ask why, someone grabs my long hair in a painful tug, and then a large knife comes into view. Fear grips me as I peer up at the mirror to take a look at who is holding the knife at my throat. He was tall, dark olive-skinned, bald, with a goat tee. His build reminded me of Mattia and Hamm, except his shoulders were broader. I glance towards the knife, which is held at my neck, and whimper. The jagged edge of the blade had blood on it and not dried blood, but fresh blood. Who had this man hurt or, worse, killed?

I look up and see him staring at me in the mirror. A wicked grin breaks out against his hard-angled face. "Your father should have known better than to screw with us. Keep your mouth shut, or you will meet the same fate as your two goons."

With a sinking feeling in my stomach, I realized that Mattia and Lucy's protector was most likely incapacitated or, worse, dead. Panic courses through me as I desperately hope that Lucy has escaped unharmed. My gaze flicks to my phone, and the sight of Giovanni frozen in terror sends shivers down my spine. The man seems oblivious to the device, but with Mattia out of commission, I need to gather as much information as possible so Giovanni can rescue me.

"What do you mean? My father is a good man."

"He put away our boss, and he is going to pay for that with your life," he says, digging the knife deeper into the skin of my throat. I feel the pain of the cut and the trickling of the blood as it dips down to my chest.

"Where are you taking me?" I ask, trying to be as brave as possible despite fear running through every nerve in my body.

"Back to the motherland, Cuba. However, I need to leave something of you behind so he knows, without a doubt, we have you," he answers as he pulls the knife back and slices.

Chapter Thirty-One

GIOVANNI

This couldn't be happening. I sit watching as the motherfucker puts the knife to Angelina's delicate skin and know there isn't a thing I can do about it. When I heard him say the two goons were not going to help, I knew Angelina was all alone.

Thankfully, the vile creature on the other end of the video call remained oblivious to my presence. My fierce and quick-thinking wife didn't give in to panic. Instead, she calmly assessed the situation and determined where the bastard was taking her. And if Cruz's men believed that Cuba would be a barrier to me finding and rescuing her, they were gravely mistaken. Nothing would stand in my way, not even the entire planet, when it came to saving my beloved wife from those who dared to lay a hand on her.

I see him raise the knife, and it takes everything I have inside of me to remain still. Angelina never takes her eyes off me, and the intensity in them would have made my knees buckle if I had been standing. As they say, eyes are the windows to the soul, and as I look into Angelina's soul, I see the love she has for me. She loves me. The blade comes down.

slicing through hand full of her beautiful hair. He raises his hand, and I see her long, white, golden locks in his fist.

"I'm leaving this piece for your father to find. The next won't be your hair," he growls as he pulls from the dressing room. I quickly dial Hamm's number as soon as they leave the room.

"Bring the car around and notify all my security. The Cubans have kidnapped Angelina from the boutique," I say, rushing through the house and out the door. Seconds later, the Bentayga slid to a stop as four black SUVs came alongside.

I run to the car and jump in. As Hamm takes off at full speed, I call Luca.

"Hey, Gio," he answers light-heartedly.

"Luca, we have a situation. The Cubans have kidnapped Angelina."

"How do you know this, and is Lucy with them?" he asks, panicking.

A wave of panic washes over me as I relay the horrifying news. "They were ambushed at the boutique," I say tremblingly. "I was talking to Angelina on a video call when it happened." My heart races as I imagine the chaos and carnage that unfolded. "Their guards are gravely injured, maybe even dead. We need to get there immediately!" I yell.

"I am leaving now and will meet you there," he says as I hear his footsteps on the floor as he runs.

"Alright," I reply.

Why did I underestimate the danger? Why didn't I send a stronger security team with her? And why did I hesitate to go after Cruz and his men, even though he was in prison? The Famiglia's long reach could have easily brought death upon that despicable fucker.

"Sir," Hamm says. "I have called the others, and they are meeting us at the boutique. I also called the police chief and made him aware of the situation. He is sending the correct officers to the scene."

"Thanks, Hamm."

Traffic is a sea of chaos, but Hamm navigates through it effortlessly, his foot barely leaving the gas pedal. We screech to a stop in front of the shop, and I burst out of the car with my gun drawn. As I kick open the front door, I am greeted by a scene of pure horror. Blood splatters on every surface and the lifeless bodies of two women lie in a pool of crimson just inches from my feet, their necks brutally slashed open. Suddenly, the door swings open again, and I whip around to face an army of Luca's men, guns pointed directly at me and Hamm. As I look at each of their determined faces, I know without a doubt we will be on the winning side.

"Fuck," Luca gasps as he takes in the room.

My heart hammers in my chest as I signal for him to go left while I silently circle to the right. My steps are cautious, every muscle tense for danger. And then I see it. Mattia's lifeless body sprawled on the ground, his neck brutally slashed just like the others. A surge of anger and fear pulses through me as I continue deeper into the building. My hand tightens around my weapon as I enter the dressing rooms, ready for a confrontation. But instead, I find myself frozen in shock at the sight before me. Angelina's phone lies abandoned on a shelf near the mirrors, her long locks strewn across the floor in a tangled mess. The sweet scent of her perfume lingers in the air, taunting me with memories of her laughter and warmth. As I pick up the hair and bring it to my nose, tears prick at my eyes, and rage boils in my veins.

"Mr. Genovese," Hamm calls out. "The building is clear."

"Did you find Lucy?" I ask.

Luca comes around the corner. "No. I found her purse and phone but not her. Do you think they took her as well?"

"I don't know."

"Mr. Genovese," one of the guards says.

"Yes."

"Justin has found the surveillance equipment."

"Show me," I demand.

He leads us toward the back of the building and into an office. Justin is sitting at the desk behind the computer screen. I walk behind him with Luca close to me. He starts the video, and we watch. Angelina and Lucy come in, and the sales ladies meet them at the door. They are laughing and having a great time. I see Angelina and Lucy walk back towards the dressing rooms. Moments later, the door opens, and four men dressed in suits walk in. The sales ladies go to them, and within seconds, they are overpowered, and their bodies drop to the ground. The men move toward Mattia and Lucy's guard, who are looking towards the back of the store. Quickly and effortlessly, they are taken out as well, never knowing what was happening.

Justin changes the cameras, and we are watching the ones that are outside of the dressing rooms. I see the man I saw in the video open the door to Angelina's dressing room. I don't need to see what happens when he does because I already have. After he cuts off her hair, he drags her from the room. One of the other men comes forward and inserts a needle in her arm. Her body goes limp, and they carry her out the back door with the other two guys following.

"They didn't take Lucy," Luca says. "So where is she?"

I keep watching the screen, and I see movement coming out of the dressing room beside the one Angelina was in. "Look, Luca."

Lucy comes out and heads out the door that the guys just went out. Where was she going?

"Justin, are there cameras in the back?"

He pushes some buttons, and the alley behind the shop appears on the screen. I see the men put Angelina's body in the back of a black SUV and take off. Moments later, Lucy emerges and runs over to a Porsche 911. She opens the door and gets in. We watch as she ducks down, and moments later, she takes off.

"Fuck, she just hotwired that car?" I say.

"Yeah, she is really good at it. Do you think she is following the SUV?" Lucas asks.

"I'm sure of it. Justin, can you run the plate and get the VIN? Then tap into the car's GPS."

Justin's fingers fly over the keys. As we wait, Davide, Danti, and Andrea rush in. "What the fuck is going on?' Davide asks.

"Matteo Cruz's men kidnapped Angelina and killed everyone else except for Lucy. She is following their vehicle in a hotwired car," I explain.

"What the fuck?" Davide growls. "How the hell does she know how to hotwire a car? Luca, you need to lock her up somewhere before she gets herself killed."

"You know how difficult she can be," Luca says.

"Well, marry her ass off to a man who can control if you can't," Davide says through gritted teeth.

Luca steps closer to Davide. "And who do you think can control her? You?"

"Yes," he replies, his eyes never leaving Luca's.

"I got her," Justin says.

"Where is she?"

"She just came out of Lincoln tunnel and got on 495. I bet they are taking Mrs. Genovese to Newark Airport," Justin says.

"It would make sense. They must have a private jet if they will take her back to Cuba," Hamm says.

"Alright, we need to get there ASAP," I say.

"We won't get there in time. We need to slow down their departure," Luca declares.

My mind races as I try to think of Angelina in the hands of those motherfuckers. I am a founding son of The Famiglia, the most powerful organization in the world. We have members everywhere, including the FAA. "Davide, call Jack Carter and have him delay the flight. Make sure he tells his air traffic controls to give them some plausible explanation."

"Great ideal." Davide pulls out his phone and calls the

head of FAA, Jack Carter. He was helpful many times when they needed to fly out or in under the radar. We rush out of the shop and climb into our vehicles. Luca, Davide, and Justin get in the car with me, while Danti and Andrea get in the other vehicle.

"Where is Lucy now?" I ask.

"She is speeding down 495 to I-95," Justin answers, pointing to the screen.

I clench my fist, frustrated that I can't communicate with her. "Why didn't she take her purse or at least her phone?" I look over to Luca, who is holding the bag. It was a large fire engine red. Maybe she thought it would bring attention to her. When she slipped out the back door, she was wearing black leggings and a black shirt.

"I don't know, but she did take her gun," Luca says.

"Does she know how to shoot?" I ask.

Luca rubs the back of his neck. "Probably better than most of our men. She convinced Dad to teach her when she was young."

I glance back over at the screen and watch the blimp on the monitor. "Justin, is there a way we can talk to her without a phone?"

His brow furrows, a look of intense focus etched onto his face. Justin Masters was known as the mastermind of The Famiglia, his analytical mind capable of cracking any code and infiltrating even the most secure systems without leaving a single trace behind. He was a valuable asset to the organization, feared by their enemies and respected by his peers.

"The Porsche 911 has a smart chip which connects to a satellite wifi. If I can locate the transponder number, I can reverse the connection, and we should be able to talk to Lucy," he states as his fingers dance across the keys.

As I gaze out the window, the bustling city below feels like a completely different world from the one I occupy. My mind is consumed with images of Angelina's terrified face as she was held at knifepoint. Despite my status as Don of the powerful Genovese crime family, I couldn't save her at that moment. The weight of my power and responsibility crushes me, knowing it wasn't enough to protect someone I care for. No, not care for. I love her. I love her with all my heart and soul. She will never know if we can't get to her in time.

"I got it," Justin says. "Lucy Gambino, this is Justin Masters."

"Justin, how are you doing this," she says.

"Lulu," Lucas says, his voice heavy with emotion.

"Lu, where are you?" she asks.

"I am in Giovanni's car coming toward you," he answers. "Why did you hotwire that car?"

"Because Angelina is my friend, I wouldn't allow those bastards to take her. We wouldn't know which airport they were taking her if I didn't follow her."

"You should have taken grabbed your fucking phone," Davide growls.

"I only had a few seconds, and I grabbed the first thing I could put my hands on," she snaps back.

"From now on, Lucida Esmeralda Gambino, you will carry your phone with you at all times, and if you don't, you will have to be punished," Davide barks.

"By you? You are not the boss of me?" she says.

"Not yet," Davide replies with a smirk.

Holy shit, I think Davide has just made his intentions known. Lucy Gambino was going to be his.

Chapter Thirty-Two

GIOVANNI

A fiery inferno rages within me as I near Newark Airport. Drago's cage door is flung open, and he stands ready to unleash his wrath upon the Cuban scum, reducing them to nothing but piles of smoldering ash.

"Lucy, what is going on?" Luca asks. I know he is worried about his high-strung sister.

"They just turned into the private plane hangars. I'm three cars back," she answers.

"Do you know which hangar they are going to?" I ask.

"Hold on, Gio," she replies.

Every second feels like an eternity as I eagerly await Lucy's answer. My heart pounds with fear and anticipation, knowing my beloved Angelina's fate rests in her hands. If I can only get her back, I vow to never let her out of my sight again, surrounding her with armed guards at all times. She is my everything, and I will do whatever it takes to keep her safe.

"They are pulling into the third hangar from the entrance," Lucy says.

"Alright. Now turn that car around and get the fuck out of there," Davide commands.

"Listen here, Mr. Bonanno, you are not my father or

brother, and I don't have to obey your commands. I'm going to park on the backside of hangar one and wait for you guys to get here," Lucy growls.

"Lucy...Lucy," Davide calls out before yelling into the phone. "LUCY GAMBINO!" Davide's jaw is clenched so tight that he might break a tooth.

The only sound I hear is the closing of the door. "Justin, where is she?"

"The car is stopped behind hangar one. The connection is still active, but it seems she is not in the vehicle," he answers.

"How long until we get there?" I ask.

"Twenty minutes, sir," Hamm answers.

"Can't we go any faster?"

"We are going as fast as we can," Hamm says.

The tension in the car becomes palpable as the minutes tick by. The engine roars and the tires screech against the asphalt, desperate to propel us forward. The urgency in our hearts is matched only by the fervor in our souls. Angelina, my beloved wife, is in danger, and we must reach her before it's too late.

As the car hurtles down the highway, my mind races with thoughts of Angelina. Memories of our time together flash before my eyes like a rapid succession of film frames. She completely engulfs me with her laughter, touch, and contemplative nature, igniting desperation and determination.

I clench my fists, feeling the adrenaline pumping through my veins. The road blurs before me, a mere backdrop to the overwhelming need to protect the woman I love.

Luca's knuckles turn white as he makes a fist. His eyes flicker with a combination of worry and steely resolve. Beside him, Davide's hands tremble with barely contained rage. He murmurs, Nevermore over and over again. His own demon, The Raven, is released from his cage.

We are united not by blood but by loyalty, each driven by our demons and the desire to keep our families safe.

The anticipation becomes unbearable, and the silence in the car is deafening. Suddenly, a wave of anxiety courses through me as I realize that time is running out.

"We're here," Hamm announces as the car screeches to a halt. I throw open the door and rush towards hangar three, my heart pounding in my chest. Luca and Davide are hot on my heels, as well as the others in the other vehicles.

The adrenaline in my system has me moving faster than I've ever moved before, every step a testament to my desperation. Drago is clawing out to find justice for hurting our love, Angelina.

Outside the hangar's door, I pause for all the men to catch up. With silent instructions, I direct them to different locations around the hangar. Giving them a moment to get into position, I slowly opened the door and was shocked by what I saw.

Inside the hangar, the chaos is overwhelming. The air is thick with smoke, and screams echo in the distance. I see two of the men firing toward the back of the hangar. Who were they firing at? Suddenly, two shots ring out, and the two Cubans drop to the ground. Each of them received a precise shot between their eyes. Whoever the shooter had one hell of an aim.

I motion for the others to spread out. Staying in the shadows, we maneuver the outer walls of the hangar. The plane's steps are down, but I see no movement inside. We know four men took Angelina. However, we must find out how many more could be waiting for them with the plane.

My heart races as I move cautiously through the hangar, adrenaline coursing through my veins. My eyes land on the lifeless body of one of Angelina's captors, a bullet hole between his eyes. Suddenly, a deafening gunshot rings out, and I feel a rush of wind as it narrowly misses me. My head snapped back to see the final scumbag, the one who held a knife to Angelina's neck, crumpled to the ground. Without hesitation, I spin around to find my savior and am shocked to see none other than Lucy Gambino, her gun still smoking in her hand.

She presses a finger to her lips, signaling me to follow her towards the black SUV. My heart races as I rush to the back door and yank it open. As I peer inside, my breath catches in my throat. There, lying on the seat is my beloved Angelina. She lies still and pale, but I refuse to believe she's gone. With trembling hands, I reach for her wrist and frantically search for a pulse. When I finally feel a faint but steady beat beneath my fingertips, relief floods through me. She's alive, and I thank whoever may be listening for sparing her life. "Angelina, open those beautiful eyes for me?"

"Giovanni," she mumbles.

Hearing her voice allows me to breathe for the first time since she was taken. "Yes, my love."

Her eyes open and she gives me a small smile. "You found me."

"Always," I say, meaning it with my life. Lucy comes up beside me. She closes her eyes again and sighs. Whatever the fuckers gave her needs to be washed out of her system.

"Is she okay?" Lucy asks.

"Yes, thanks to you," I answer. "Is there anyone else?"

"No. They didn't expect anyone to find them so quickly."

"You know your brother is going to be pissed," I say as I pick up Angelina and cradle her in my arms.

"Yeah," she says and motions toward Angelina. "But she is worth his wrath."

I inhale her scent and sigh. "Thank you for being such a good friend."

"Always. Now let's get her to a doctor," Lucy says, putting her gun in the back of her pants.

I pull Angelina closer and quickly walk across the hangar. Luca, Davide, Andrea, and Danti meet us. Davide steps forward and looks Lucy over. He takes a deep breath and holds it for several moments before letting out.

When did this happen? Davide wasn't upset that his friend's sister didn't obey her brother's command. No, Davide was upset because he had feelings for Lucy Gambino.

He takes a step closer to Lucy. "Are you okay?" he asks in a voice for of concern and something else.

Lucy, the strong, confident woman who had just taken out four Cuban corporation members by herself with a handgun, ducks her head. Each shot is given with pinpoint accuracy for one result only, a kill shot.

"I'm fine. We need to get Angelina to a doctor. So can we get out of here, please?" she asks.

Davide looks at her and nods. "But we are going to talk about this shit later."

"Giovanni, we need to get her to the hospital," Andrea says. "The doc is waiting at Kings County. The helicopter will be landing in five."

"You got a copter?" I asked. How had he pulled this off so fucking fast? He gives me a wink.

"Always have a backup plan," Andrea says with a smirk. "Now, let's get her on board."

We carefully lay Angelina on the stretcher, securing her in place. The deafening sound of the helicopter blades whirring above us fills the air as we rush her toward the waiting aircraft. The urgency of the situation fuels our movements, and as I climb aboard, I can't help but feel a glimmer of hope amidst the chaos.

The flight to Kings County Hospital is a blur, my focus solely on Angelina's delicate form lying before me. Her face, usually radiating with warmth and life, now appears fragile and pale. The weight of responsibility settles heavily on my shoulders, knowing it is up to me to protect her from further harm.

As we touch down at the hospital helipad, medical staff swarm the helicopter, ready to whisk Angelina away for immediate treatment. I watch helplessly as they rush her through the doors, disappearing.

"Giovanni."

I turn to find Charles standing behind me. I had forgotten all about him during the drama. Fuck, how insensitive of me. "Charles."

His face is pale, and his face looks as if he had aged ten years. "Is she...is she alive?"

I step closer and place my hand on his shoulder. "Yes. The motherfuckers injected her with something to knock her out. We own this hospital, and she is in the best hands in the world."

"We own this hospital?" Charles asks with narrowed eyes.

"Yes, this is one of the hospitals The Famiglia own."

"Mr. Genovese, Mr. Greco, come with me to the lounge where you can wait," a smartly dressed woman says.

We follow her through the hospital until we reach a large room. I see Hamm and another guard by the door. Even though we are in a Famiglia and security is top-notch, I need to ensure it is increased. I will never make that mistake again.

Hamm opens the door, and I find my friends waiting for me when I step inside. Not only my fellow leaders but also Nan, Lucy, Anna, Zoey, and Aunt Athena, with faces full of concern. Charles and I walk over and take a seat on the small couch.

"If you need anything, just ask. The nurses will keep you up to date on Mrs. Genovese's progress," the woman says.

"Thank you," I say.

Charles and I are handed cups of coffee. Take a sip of cheap, hot coffee and think about how I would make the rest of Matteo Cruz's organization disappear.

I gather my thoughts, staring into the depths of the steaming liquid before me. Matteo Cruz and his organization had gone too far this time. They had taken Angelina, the woman I loved, and harmed her in ways that made my blood boil. No longer would I sit idly by and let them continue their reign of terror. It was time to take action.

As the bitter taste of the coffee lingered on my tongue, I made a silent promise to myself. I would tear down every piece of Cruz's empire brick by brick until no trace remained. And I would do it for Angelina.

Nan's voice breaks through my thoughts, pulling me back to the present. "Giovanni, we're here for you," she says softly, her eyes filled with empathy.

I nod in acknowledgment, grateful for their support. The room falls into a heavy silence as we wait anxiously for any news about Angelina's condition. Time feels stagnant, with each passing moment stretched thin until we finally receive an update from the nurse. As she approaches, her face is a mixture of concern and relief.

"Mr. Genovese, your wife is stable. The doctors were able to reverse the effects of the substance in her system, and she is waking up now. We'll keep you updated on her condition as we receive more information," the nurse explains calmly, her professional demeanor a stark contrast to the chaos that had just unfolded.

As Charles and I stand, we exchange glances, our eyes filled with relief and determination. The Famiglia will find and punish those responsible for this horrific act. But for now, we will focus on helping Angelina recover. We thank the nurse and make our way to Angelina's room, ready to be by her side as she awakens from this nightmare.

In the quiet moments of our wait, I reflect on the events that have led us to this point. The constant struggle against rival factions, the battles fought, the lives lost. It's a life filled with danger and uncertainty, but the only life I've ever known. And amid all the chaos, I find solace in knowing I have a loyal family.

As we enter Angelina's room, the soft beeping of the monitors fills the air. She lies in the hospital bed, her eyes fluttering open as she slowly regains consciousness. Seeing her awake brings a rush of relief and joy that washes over me.

"Angelina," I breathe her name, my voice filled with emotion. "You're safe now."

Her gaze meets mine, and a faint smile tugs at the corners of her lips. "Giovanni," Her voice is weak but full of gratitude.

I take her hand in mine, cherishing the warmth that radiates from her touch.

Chapter Thirty-Three

ANGELINA

I am never so glad to be home. I spent three days in the hospital, having the drugs washed out of my system. My first question was Lucy was okay. Giovanni explained how she was the one who saved me. The thought of her hot-wiring a car and shooting all the bad guys made me smile.

My father spent many hours by my bed. The pain of what could have happened was painted on his features. Giovanni reassured him that Matteo Cruz's days were numbered, as were all those who worked for him. I didn't know how Giovanni could do that, but I knew Giovanni didn't make fake promises.

Giovanni opens the door and helps me out of the car. His strong, large arm wraps around my waist, and we slowly walk up the steps to the front door. Margaret and several members of the staff are waiting with smiles.

"Welcome home, Mrs. Genovese," Margaret says.

"Margaret, please, for the last time, call me Angelina."

She looks towards Giovanni, who gives her a smile and a nod. "Welcome home, Angelina."

The staff was full of warm and friendly faces, but Margaret stands out as my favorite. Her gentle smile and soothing voice comfort everyone who crosses her path. It wasn't until I got to know her better that I learned the tragic story of her past. At the young age of twenty-one, she lost her husband while he was involved with the Genovese crime family. Despite this heart-wrenching loss, she found solace in working for Giovanni's father within the safety of his home. The walls seemed to whisper secrets of her pain and resilience, making her even more beloved by all.

We walk in, and Giovanni walks us towards the stairs. "Where are we going?" I ask.

"I'm taking you to our bedroom," he replies. "I'll have lunch brought up."

I didn't want to go to bed. "Can we sit outside for a little while? I think the fresh air and sunshine would do me some good."

He sighs, and I can see he is having a hard time granting my request. Just when I thought we were going upstairs, he turned us, and we walked towards the den, where the French doors led to a lovely garden. It was one of my favorite spots, with large trees, perfectly manicured shrubs, and brightly colored flowers. A large water fountain glistened in the center of the garden, its gentle sounds providing a soothing backdrop to our conversation. Giovanni guides me towards a cozy bench nestled under the shade of a towering oak tree.

We sit down, and I take a moment to breathe in the familiar scents of the flowers, letting their fragrance wash away the remnants of my time in captivity. Giovanni places his arm around my shoulders, drawing me closer to him as we watch the sunlight dance through the leaves overhead.

"I'm glad we came out here," he murmurs, leaning his head against mine. "You've been through so much, Angelina. I wish I could take it all away."

I intertwine my fingers with his fingers, finding solace in his touch. "Being here with you is enough," I whisper. "Knowing that we're safe and together."

Giovanni's gaze is filled with tenderness as he looks at me, his eyes tracing the contours of my face. "I'll do whatever it takes to protect you, Angelina. I won't let anyone ever hurt you again."

His words bring a wave of warmth and comfort, soothing the lingering fears that still haunt me. Giovanni has always been my protector, my rock in the storm. And now, more than ever, I realize how much I need him by my side.

As we sit there in the tranquil garden, time seems to stand still. The worries and troubles of the outside world fade away, leaving only the two of us and our shared love. Giovanni's presence envelops me like a shield, shielding me from the darkness threatening to consume us.

"I don't want to let fear dictate our lives," I say softly, breaking the peaceful silence between us. "We've been through so much already, but I refuse to let it define us."

Giovanni's eyes sparkle with admiration as he gazes at me. "You've always had a strength within you, Angelina. It's what drew me to you from the very beginning. You have an unmatched resilience, and I do not doubt that we can overcome anything together."

I lean my head against his chest, listening to the steady rhythm of his heartbeat. "I never thought I would find someone like you," I admit, my voice barely above a whisper. "Someone who understands and accepts me for who I am."

Giovanni's arms tighten around me, holding me close. "And I never thought I would find someone as brave, as beautiful, as you," he murmurs, his words laced with sincerity. "You've brought light into my life, Angelina. A light that shines even in the darkest of times. Angelina, I love you."

My eyes fill with tears, sparkling like diamonds in the light, as his words wash over me. The weight of his love settles deep within my heart, warming every corner and filling me with indescribable joy. It's a feeling I never thought I would experience hearing those three simple words from his lips. My hand reaches up, trembling slightly, to caress his face. The face of the man who has captured my heart and soul. Every crease and line is etched into my memory, a map of our journey together. And in that moment, as our gazes lock, I know without a doubt that this love will endure any storm that may come our way.

At that moment, everything fades away except for the two of us. The world stands still as I gaze into Giovanni's eyes, overwhelmed by the love and adoration shining within them. My heart swells with emotions I never thought possible, and I can't help but let the tears spill over.

"I love you too, Giovanni," I whisper, my voice quivering with sincerity. "More than words can express."

He leans closer, his lips brushing against mine in a gentle, tender kiss. It's a kiss filled with the weight of all that we've been through, all the pain and uncertainty that has brought us to this point. But it's also a kiss that holds so much promise and hope, a promise of a future where we can finally be free from the shadows that have haunted us.

As we pull away, Giovanni brushes away my tears with his thumb, his touch comforting and grounding. "We've faced the worst together," he says softly. "Now it's time to build the life we've always dreamed of. A life filled with love, happiness, and a future that knows no bounds."

I nod, feeling a renewed sense of determination coursing through my veins. "I believe in us, Giovanni," I say, my voice steady and unwavering. "No matter what comes our way, we'll face it together."

Giovanni's eyes shine with a mixture of pride and adoration as he looks at me. "Together," he repeats, his voice filled with conviction.

We sit in the garden, basking in the sunlight and the warmth of each other's presence. It's a moment of pure serenity and tranquility, a respite from the chaos surrounding us for far too long. In this sacred space, we find solace and peace, knowing that we have each other to lean on as we navigate the unpredictable journey of life.

As we sit there, lost in our thoughts and dreams, a gentle breeze rustles through the oak tree leaves, carrying a sense of hope and renewal. At that moment, I couldn't help but feel grateful for everything that had led us to this point. The pain and darkness of the past are slowly fading away, replaced by the warmth and love that Giovanni brings into my life.

We spend hours in that garden, discussing our dreams and aspirations and sharing our deepest fears and insecurities. Giovanni listens with unwavering support, constantly reminding me that I am never alone. Together, we forge a path forward, determined to create a future filled with joy and fulfillment.

Days turn into weeks, and weeks turn into months. Life begins to settle into a new rhythm where danger and uncertainty no longer loom over us. Giovanni's promises hold true as Matteo Cruz is killed in prison. No one knows who did it, but I feel sure Giovanni knows. Matteo's criminal empire crumbled under the weight of The Famiglia.

Even though the threat from the Cuban Organization was over, it didn't mean Giovanni loosened his demands for security for me. I have a team of six guards with me whenever I leave home. At first bucked over having so many, but that got me my ass spanked red. It wasn't until I was over his lap I understood why. Giovanni loved me, and he would do anything to keep me safe.

Today, my team of guards and I were on our way to Bella Luna for lunch with Lucy. We haven't had a chance to get together after my kidnapping. Her father and mother wanted her to come to Italy for a visit. I think it was because of what she did to save me. I asked Giovanni if that was the case. He assured me I wasn't the reason. However, I knew he wasn't telling me something.

We pulled up in front of the restaurant, and when the

team felt it was safe, they opened the door for me. When I stepped out, I was immediately surrounded. We walk in, and I smile when I see a male host at the podium.

"Hello, Mrs. Genovese. Miss Gambino is already at your table," he says with a smile. "Please follow me."

I navigate through the bustling restaurant, feeling the weight of hundreds of eyes on me. They all whisper and stare, desperate to know who I am, the wife of one of the world's most powerful and feared men. My heart races as I pass by, trying to maintain a composed facade while inwardly screaming at the suffocating attention. Giovanni's constant reassurance of how strong I was and how proud he was of me.

"Angelina," Lucy says as she stands and pulls me into a tight hug.

"Lucy," I cry, holding her tight. This woman was the reason why I was alive. Over the last few months, I handled what happened to me surprisingly well, except for a few times when it all came back in a crush detail.

We pull apart and I motion for her to take a seat. "You look great," I say.

"Thank you. I love your hair," she says.

I run my fingers through my newly chopped hair, which now falls just below my shoulders. The kidnapper had hacked off chunks of it, leaving an uneven mess. But Giovanni immediately called in a top hairstylist from New York to fix the damage. He always loved my long locks, especially when he would grab handfuls of them while thrusting deep inside me. I promised to grow it back, but he insisted I keep it short when I mentioned that I've been having fewer headaches without the weight. With a cocky smile, he reminded me that there was still plenty to pull on during sex, and I couldn't resist dropping to my knees to give him a mind-blowing blow job.

"Yeah, I love it. So tell me all about Italy," I say.

"It was good," she replies, though I notice her face doesn't match her comment.

"As tradition dictates, the virginity test will still be adminis-
tered before the wedding. However, in a break from tradition,
no witness will be present. The grand ceremony must still take
place in the esteemed Famiglia chapel, and the marking ritual
must be completed. But the couple will finally have some
much-needed privacy for the highly anticipated wedding
night. Once the union is consummated, The Commission will
await the presentation of the sheet as evidence of their official
union."

I go from face to face, reading their thoughts. The
founding sons and the newest member, Theo Croft, agreed
with the proposed rule change. Jackson, Sidney, and Lee
debate the merits of the possible change.

I watch the others in The Commission exchange glances
and open their mouths to speak. It's a tense moment, and I
brace myself for a potential backlash. But then, one by one,
they nod in agreement.

"Alright, then," Luca says, still with a hint of skepticism.
"We will vote on this. All in favor of the rule change, say, aye."

A chorus of ayes fills the room, and I can't help but smile.
This change won't truly end the tradition, but it will bring a
bit of light into the darkness for the new brides of The
Famiglia.

As we continue our meeting, discussing other issues that
plague our organization, I feel more hopeful for the future.
Progress is difficult and often met with resistance, but slow and
steady change can eventually bring about a better organization.

"Giovanni."

As I lift my gaze, my heart stutters and thrums in my chest.
Standing in the doorway, radiating beauty and light, is the one
who holds my soul captive - Angelina. Her eyes sparkle with
mirth as she smiles and glides towards me. Without hesitation,
I pull her onto my lap, and she lets out a tinkling laugh, like
the chime of a bell on a gentle breeze. The warmth of her

body against mine wraps me in a cocoon of love and contentment.

"Did you have a good lunch?" I ask.

"I did," she replied with a warm smile, but I couldn't help but notice the subtle furrowing of her brow. Her expression held a hint of concern, as if there was more to the story than she was letting on.

I gently place my hand on her cheek, my fingers tracing the delicate curve of her jawline as I gaze into her troubled eyes. "My love, what is troubling you?" I inquire, hoping to ease the crease between her eyebrows and bring a spark back into her weary expression.

"Lucy told me Luca has found her a husband."

"Yeah, I know," I reply. "It is a solid match, and he will treat her right."

"Giovanni, she is in love with someone. She will never be happy without him. Can't you talk to Luca and see if you can change his mind?" Angelina asks.

"Did she tell you who this man is that she loves?" I ask.

I was confident of the man she would marry, and despite his reluctance to admit it, I could sense the strong emotions he held for her. But hidden beneath his facade of indifference were raw, primal desires that kept him from acting upon his true feelings. He struggled with his inner demons. The men in his family, for generations, had indulged in extramarital affairs. He was afraid he would inherit the gene. His father fucked around his entire marriage to Nan. He never really talked about it because tough Mafia Dons don't speak about their feelings with others. However, I could tell it had a profound effect on how he viewed marriage.

"She wouldn't tell me. I think she is just overwhelmed with all of it. I guess she is lucky she doesn't have to marry a founding son," Angelia says.

I was going to upset her by telling her that it was, in fact, a founding son Lucy was engaged to.

With a gentle pull, I draw Angelina closer and breathe in her intoxicating scent. The warmth of her body against mine fills me with a sense of contentment and gratitude - it's not every day one finds their soulmate, let alone someone who shares the same powerful dragon living within them. My lovely wife is a perfect match for my inner beast, and I can't help but feel like the luckiest bastard alive. Though she may seem delicate and graceful on the outside, I know that beneath that exterior lies a fierce dragon waiting to defend its host. It only emerged once before when a rude hostess at Bella Luna dared to challenge her, but I have no doubt it will reappear whenever she needs its protection.

"Maybe they will be as lucky as we were," I say.

"Maybe."

I gingerly place my hand on her stomach, feeling the slight curve of her abdomen beneath my fingers. We had just received the news that she was pregnant, and I couldn't help but feel a mixture of excitement and nervousness coursing through me. "How are you feeling?" I ask, my voice filled with a sense of awe as I gaze at her with love and wonder in my eyes. The realization of new life growing inside her fills me with an overwhelming sense of joy and responsibility.

"Despite the constant cravings and exhaustion, I'm doing well," she replies with a slight sigh, snuggled up against my chest. Her breath is warm against my skin as she nuzzles closer, seeking comfort and warmth in our embrace. Her chest's soft rise and fall matches mine, creating a soothing rhythm between us. The scent of lavender lingers on her skin, calming my restless thoughts. At this moment, I am content to simply hold her and listen to the steady beat of her heart.

"What is the craving today?"

"Peach ice cream with sardines sounds so good," she moaned.

My stomach lurched at the thought. "Why don't we go up

to our room and take a nap? I'll tell Margaret what you want, and when you wake up, it will be ready."

"You don't think it is too weird to you?" she asks, biting her lower lip.

"No, baby, I don't. You are Angelina Genovese, and you are carrying the future of The Famiglia."

I stand, gently holding her fragile body against my chest, and breathe out a contented sigh. At this moment, with her in my arms, my world feels whole and complete. The warmth of her small frame radiates through me, filling every crevice of my being with love and joy. I know that no matter what challenges lie ahead, as long as she is by my side, my life will always be full and meaningful.

The End

About the Author

Amber Joi Scott or the Wicked Writing Wench, born and raised in the South with a snarky attitude and kiss-my-ass mentality. Also, being born in the month of August, she embraces her Leo sign, letting her inner lion roar through her writing.

She lives in the beautiful Shenandoah Valley with her big, burly husband and their many animals. Raising her children to be polite, hardworking young adults is and will always be her biggest accomplishment. When deciding on her pen name, she dedicated all her writing to her children by using parts of their names as her pen name.

She doesn't plan to stop writing anytime soon and hopes that people fall in love with her characters as much as she has.

Also by Amber Joi Scott

Amber Joi Scott

In a Heartbeat

Trust and Obey

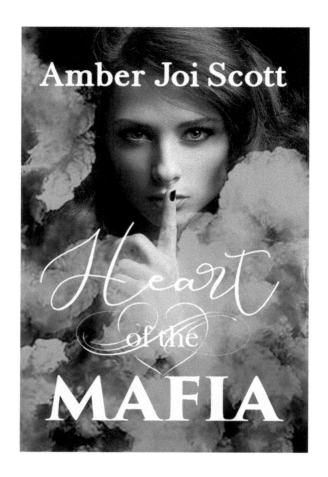

Heart of the Mafia

Wishing Upon a Snowflake

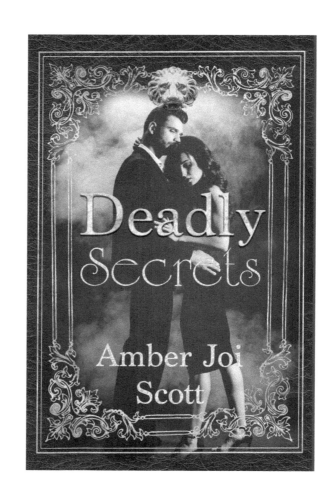

Deadly Secrets

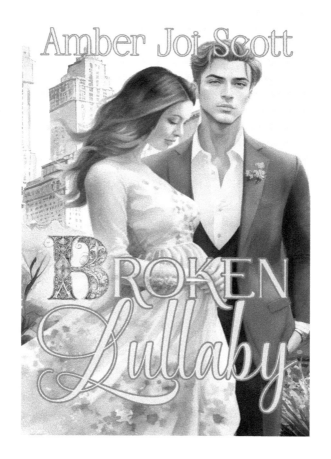

Broken Lullaby